# EMERALD BAY MURDER

## DAMIAN GREEN MYSTERY SERIES

ALEC PECHE

*This is my 26th book, due to an infection just as I was trying to cross the finish line of a completed story, I had to hustle to make up for two weeks of lost time.*

*I so appreciate the flexibility of my editor Ellen Falk to read the story in pieces so I could make my deadline. Likewise my first reader, G. Meyer gave me her time to take the book to the next level.*

*I don't know what I would have done without these two women changing their schedules to help me perfect this story.*

*All I can say is thanks and well done!*

# CHAPTER 1

*D*amian Green changed out of his wetsuit which he used to swim around his private island located in San Francisco Bay. While the island itself was about a half-mile swim, his swim ended up as about three-quarters of a mile as he had to avoid the rocks surrounding his island. He was a little above average height, lean, and Nordic or perhaps English in his appearance. He never knew his parents and hadn't bothered with DNA tests to find his heritage. He went inside to put the finishing touches on his appearance before heading into the office.

His cell phone rang, and it was Natalie Severino according to the caller ID. Natalie had solved the murder of Damian's wife and two daughters nearly a decade ago. Then she shot the suspect dead. Since that time, he'd helped her with a variety of cold cases. Damian wasn't a police officer or a private detective; instead, he was a computer genius capable of teasing out data that helped solve criminal cases for the San Jose Police Department. Natalie worked there as a retired detective solving cold cases at an amazing rate thanks to his support.

"Hi Natalie," he said with a sigh in his voice. He'd been

offered jobs with both the police department and the FBI, but he preferred tinkering with his inventions at his Richmond company warehouse. She hadn't asked for his assistance for several months, so he guessed it was time to get back in the saddle and help solve a criminal case. She was able to solve some cases by the resubmission of DNA evidence, but with this new case she needed Damian's help.

"How was your summer?"

"I won't be offended if you jump right to what you need me to do to help you solve a new case. That said, Ariana, Hermione, and I had a great summer."

Natalie laughed and said, "Damian, you'd make a great detective. You always get right to the question of the day."

"I know your son and daughter-in-law are thriving, so you must want my help on a case." Natalie's daughter-in-law worked for Damian and that kept him updated on the family activities.

"Do you ski, Damian?"

"That's a question out of left field, but the answer is yes."

"That's great news. My latest cold case, and no pun intended, was a tech executive found dead in the snow at Emerald Bay in Lake Tahoe. I don't ski, but it would be helpful to have your help if you did ski."

"I think I remember hearing about that case shortly after my family was murdered. I didn't pay any attention to it at the time. Wasn't he found on skis in an area that doesn't have skiers? Was he using cross-country skis or telemark skis?"

"I don't know anything about skis. How many types of skis are there?" Natalie asked.

"There are three basic kinds and then a few extra types for rare winter sports. So most people have downhill skis which are used to go downhill at your average ski resort. Cross-country skis are for the most part used on flat snowy paths, and tele-mark skis are a cross between the two, but they allow you to lift your heel up and walk up steep hills. So it's not inconceivable that the tech executive might have been wearing cross-country or telemark skis to run a local errand."

"What are the rarer types of skis?"

"There are very long skis that ski jumpers use, and short skis for moguls or freestyle. According to your report, what type of skis were on his feet?"

There was silence on the other end as Natalie searched for the answer to his question. Finally, she said, "I don't see the answer to that question."

"Is there a crime scene picture of his boots and skis?"

"Yes, I'll send it to you."

"Wait, it's not a gross picture, is it?"

"No, just a close-up on the feet."

"Okay." Damian waited to open the email and look at the picture when he heard the sound of a new email. He opened the attachment and had his answer.

"They're cross-country skis. So, maybe he put them on to run an errand, or maybe he was trying to get some cardio conditioning in. What were the time and cause of his death?"

"It was estimated to be sunset in March, so about six pm. The cause of death was unknown. We don't know that his death is even suspicious, other than there was no reason to die at the age of 34. There were no toxicology tests that proved a drug-related incident or any evidence of a heart attack. He died from a lack of oxygen, but they don't know why he lacked oxygen."

"That is strange. Lake Tahoe is at a higher elevation, but not one that causes altitude sickness from a lack of oxygen. What an interesting case. Did he die in California or Nevada? Were the police satisfied with the autopsy?"

"Emerald Bay is on the California side of the lake. So the El Dorado County coroner did his autopsy, then at the request of his family, his remains were moved to our medical examiner. He was found near a parking lot for the state park the next morning, and as you might imagine, his remains had to be thawed out."

"That's awful. Did his family report him missing?"

"Yes. He was in Lake Tahoe skiing and left his family behind in San Jose. According to the family interview, he loved skiing and did both downhill and cross-country. They had a condo in the city of South Lake Tahoe, and they would go there as a family when the kids were on school holidays. He would drive to Tahoe one or two times a month to ski and work from home."

"What was the name of his company?" Damian asked.

He could hear papers shuffling in the background and then Natalie said, "Sunnyside AI. It says here that it's an app for wineries."

Damian remembered the company, and it had nearly failed about a year after the death of the tech executive. He would research the company, but he remembered the name "Sunny-side" being mocked in tech circles. His memory was tickled by the fact that the company had been on the verge of some new innovation, and that died with the executive, but they must have been able to re-create the innovation as the company lived on with a new name. He would research it later.

"Was he dumped at the State Park, or did he die there?"

"Interesting that you should ask that question; he was thought to have been planted there as there were no treads from his skis in the snow around him. So there's a small chance that he could have put his ski shoes on and then pitched over dead, I suppose."

"No, that wouldn't work. He would have had to put the ski boots on at his car and then walked over to the trail and put his skis on at that point. You wouldn't get out of your car in your socks and walk over to the trailhead and slip your feet into boots that were already attached to the skis. You wouldn't do that because your feet would be cold and wet by the time you sunk them into the boots. So if there were no ski tracks around him, then he was dumped there. It wouldn't be easy to take a dead man to that area in the middle of the night and put ski boots on him and attach them to the skis."

"I think that's why it became a cold potential homicide case for the SJPD, as there was no way for him to collapse where he did and not leave any ski tracks anywhere, so it was concluded that his body was dumped."

"Okay, send me any crime scene photos, the medical examiner report, and any other relevant data and I'll see what I can do."

"Will do and thanks, Damian. As I ask with each case, are you sure you don't want to go to work for the SJPD?"

"Nope. I'd rather work for myself."

Natalie sighed over the phone, not surprised by Damian's answer, and they ended the call.

# CHAPTER 2

amian Green wore three hats: he was an entrepreneur with a warehouse and staff in Richmond, he helped the SJPD on occasion, and he was a dad to a high school senior. Like most adults, he was constantly switching hats as needs demanded throughout his day. He finished his ablutions and was ready to leave on his boat for the short journey to the Richmond marina where his vehicle was parked. From there he had a short ten-minute drive to his warehouse.

It was fall, and he was putting the final touches on two inventions as he planned to have them displayed at the Consumer Electronics Show, or the CES as it was known in Las Vegas, in January. While he had visited the show as a consumer, this was the first time his company was demonstrating one of his inventions. Since he was an intensely private person, he actually had two of his engineers hosting his booth at the show. If there was interest from a manufacturing company, he would license said company the rights to his two inventions. He didn't want to expand his company into the mass productions of his ideas; rather, he wanted to invent stuff and make his income on the royalties.

He had rented a house in Vegas for himself, his girlfriend, Ariana Knowles, and their ward, Hermione. He wanted to browse the show to see if it would stimulate any ideas for his company to work on but also have a space to retreat to from the noise and atmosphere of the Las Vegas strip. The three of them planned to visit the Grand Canyon and take in a few shows. School would be back in session after the Christmas break, but Hermione was an excellent student, and they had worked out her school absence in advance. Her school wasn't happy about her missing classes, but they couldn't argue much as she was a straight A student, and they had given the school nearly four months' advance notice about the absence. They also worked out the absence with her coach, as she would be missing the first week of swimming practice.

He pulled up to his warehouse with his mind on multiple tasks. His firm comprised engineers and mathematicians and also included two ex-cons. When he looked at it from the outside, it was a strange collection of people and skills, and they worked well together; but in thinking about the upcoming CES show, he knew he needed to add another person. His company had been in stealth mode as it worked on tweaking their inventions. Now, they were going public with said inventions. He needed to add a marketing person to help with the materials for the show. He'd start by asking his staff if they knew of anyone to fit that position. He'd already scheduled a staff meeting, so this was just another agenda item.

His staff was gathered around the conference table when he arrived, discussing their lives with each other. As usual he went through a progress update on each of the projects they were working on. Then he got to his new agenda item.

"I'm looking at hiring someone with a marketing background to help us prepare for CES. We need to trick out our booth and have the appropriate materials available to share with people browsing the show. That said, we don't have full-time permanent work for such an individual, so I may look at hiring a company to do an approximate four-month contract. Do you have any ideas about the position or a person to fulfill this need?"

The consensus from his staff and in particular Chris and Haley, who would be hosting their booth, was agreement with his plan. Then Lily, a mathematician and former convicted bank robber, said, "I might know of someone."

Damian raised an eyebrow at her to say, "Go on."

"I'm acquainted with my child's friends' parents at school. One of the moms was let go from her marketing position when she mentioned that she was in the early stages of her second pregnancy. I think she's three months along. She plans to stay at home with the baby after it's born, so she's not looking for long-term employment. I'm not sure what exactly her marketing job was. All I know is that I'll try and avoid ever doing business with her old employer. I know she briefly debated suing the company for discrimination, but it wasn't worth her time and money. Would you like me to find her on LinkedIn and see what her background is?"

"Thanks, Lily, just give me her name and I'll research her. I do like that her timeline matches ours," Damian said, and the meeting ended shortly thereafter with Damian planning to research Lily's contact.

After looking the woman up on various platforms, he decided she had the experience he was looking for and he had one more question for Lily.

"Your contact looks like she has the right background for what I'm looking for. I'm wondering if it would be better for me to cold-call her, or for you to reach out to her through your kid connection."

"I'll contact her and set up an appointment for tomorrow for you to interview her. Will you be here all day, or is there a time you're not available?"

"I'll be available all day."

Lily nodded, and a short time later he had an appointment set up with Emily for the next day. With his business questions resolved for the day, he took some time to review the materials that Natalie sent him. He'd told her in the past that he really didn't want to see pictures of dead bodies. In this collection of attachments she'd edited out the man's face. He was grateful for that adjustment as it allowed him to concentrate on the photos of the scene while trying to figure out the logistics of it.

The photos were dated, so he started by checking the weather of the day and night in question. There was no new snow from the estimated time of death to the discovery of his body the next morning. He also checked the winds which could be fierce in the Sierra Nevada mountains. However, there was almost no wind overnight. So the snow around his body was likely undisturbed. There were footsteps around his body, but it was another hiker/skier that found him, and then there were EMS and cops on the scene, so the footprints meant nothing.

Still he knew of no skier ever who walked through snow holding their skis and boots and then put wet and cold feet into ski boots. Instead, you sat on the edge of your seat or vehicle and put your boots on, transferring dry and warm feet from shoes to boots. He supposed that his ski boot pattern could have been trampled by first responders on the scene, except his car wasn't nearby, so he had to arrive from somewhere but there was no pattern of the skis on the snow behind him. For that reason alone, he thought the death was suspicious.

Then came the next question—how did he die? How could two medical examiners fail to determine a cause of death? He had no medical training himself, so he couldn't begin to speculate on what could cause someone's death and go undetected.

He set that aside and looked into the tech executive's

company. Who was he and what did he do for the company? His victim, John Baldwin, was a married father of two children. He was listed as the chief engineer, which was a way of saying he likely invented the piece of technology that was being used by the company. In the earliest reports of his death, he was referred to as a founder. More recently, the company referred to him as one of its engineers.

Then he looked further and saw that Mr. Baldwin's widow, Sara, was suing the company for her husband's share of the Initial Public Offering (or IPO) revenue generated shortly after his death. The court case had dragged on for years as the tech company tried to negate her husband's contribution to its success. It seemed like they were wearing her down and she might lose in the next month or two. She'd received a life insurance policy, but that was minuscule compared to the proceeds of the IPO that her husband would have received had he been alive. Now, Damian wanted to solve the case as much as for the widow as for Natalie.

He continued reading the reports that Natalie forwarded to him. He didn't see anything relevant there to solving the case. The medical examiners concluded he died from hypothermia which is kind of obvious if you're going to lie in the snow overnight. However, they had no explanation for why he was lying in the snow. They could see nothing in his body that would cause him to one moment be outside cross-country skiing and at the next moment be unconscious with the opportunity to die from hypothermia. He found notes from a detective that, in an oral conversation with the medical examiner, it was speculated that potassium could cause such a death, but there was no evidence of how it was consumed. There were some symptoms of excessive potassium, but due to the length of time between death and the post-mortem examination, and exposure to freezing temperatures, it was hard to confirm that finding.

Damian felt better for finding that possibility as he lacked the medical knowledge to understand how someone as young as the executive could die leaving so little evidence. Now he had information to understand why the case was ruled as indeterminate and he was determined to find answers for both Natalie and the dead man's widow, Sara. He switched focus to the court case for the IPO proceeds to understand how he might help her. In his mind, it was more important to help her first than to solve the unusual death of her husband.

He did a deep dive into the company that took him all the way to lunch. He decided to email Natalie to inform her that he was interested in assisting John Baldwin's widow's court case first as it was a ticking time bomb, whereas solving John murder—and he was convinced it was murder, would happen afterward.

He spent the afternoon working on his company's issues before heading back to his island. He was dining with Ariana and Hermione that evening around 6:30 pm as Hermione had after-school practice for her sport of the quarter, which was water polo. Hermione was already one of the school's best water polo players and likely at the end of this season, she would be offered college scholarships for the sport.

He took care of tasks around his house and then took out his boat for the ride across the bay to Ariana's house in the town of Belvedere. Damian felt lucky to have the two women in his life. He had closed himself off from the outside world after his wife and two children were murdered almost a decade ago by a prisoner from Soledad State Prison. The prisoner was sentenced to Soledad for the gang murders of two people. He was mistakenly released and fled north to San Jose, coming upon Damian's wife and daughters. Despite the fact that his wife gave the prisoner everything he asked for, he still turned around and murdered them in cold blood. Natalie Severino had been the lead detective on the case and was able to tract the prisoner down and shot him dead. Damian was grateful that action saved him from what would have been a very emotionally painful trial.

Damian had built his house on Red Rock Island with the thought that he would keep the outside world out and invent things in his underground lab. He earned royalties on his inventions which left him with more money than he knew what to do with. First, Ariana washed up on his island when she miscalculated the air in her scuba tank. Using a drone, he lifted her tank and refilled it so she could swim home. She in return sent him a box of his preferred tea in thanks and dropped it by a drone onto his island. She was a widow who had lost her husband to cancer, and was a venture capitalist funding start-ups in Silicon Valley.

Hermione was thirteen when she escaped from her home where her parents were kidnapped. She'd traveled over land and eventually ended up in the marina where Damian's boat was docked. She'd fallen asleep under some tarps and woken up when they reached his island. She held him at knifepoint before deciding to trust him. He called Ariana, feeling like he needed a woman to help him deal with the mysterious female teenager.

They formed a little family unit as all of them recovered from the grief of losing someone close to them. In Hermione's case, she was eventually reunited with her real parents who turned out to be in a witness protection program. However, she made the decision to stay with Damian and Ariana where she would have the freedom to live her life yet be protected by Damian's sophisticated security systems. She had occasional video calls with her parents, and they were sent transmissions of her academic and athletic achievements. Hermione reminded him of one of his daughters, and her presence filled his heart.

As usual, when he was crossing San Francisco Bay, he thought of his original family versus his new family. He thought each would approve of the other. After years of grieving, he was finally moving on with his life thanks to Ariana and Hermione. He had purpose, he helped put many bad people behind bars, he helped people with his inventions, and he kept prisoners behind bars, so no family had to suffer what he had suffered as the result of a mistake by the state prison system.

Okay, it was time to move on from his gruesome thoughts and think about the evening ahead. He wondered how the day had gone for Ariana and Hermione. He wanted to update Ariana about his potential hire of a marketing person. They had discussed it previously when he had been talking about the Vegas show. One of Ariana's start-ups would also be making an appearance, and she thought they were better prepared than Damian's company was for the show. She would be pleased he had a potential solution.

He docked his boat and grabbed his overnight bag. He and Ariana slept together when their schedules allowed it and today was such a day. He would have to stop by his island on the way to work the next day to feed his cats, but that was a minor inconvenience to enjoying Ariana's company.

He walked inside and was first greeted by Miguel, Ariana's Portuguese water dog. Once he got over giving the dog a rub, he moved on to hug and kiss Ariana.

"How was your day?" she asked.

"I had a conversation with Natalie so that was sad, and I have a potential solution to our CES show prep, so that was good."

"Explain."

Damian explained the death of the tech CEO and the lawsuit with his widow as well as the situation with the friend of Lily.

"My husband obviously knew he was dying, and he had an attorney create a sophisticated trust. One of his former partners tried something after Jared passed away and he not only lost, he got fired from the company as the other partners respected Jared's contribution to the company. I guess this other firm has fewer ethics," Ariana mused.

"And his death was unexpected at 34, so no protection for the widow from an in-depth legal consultation like you had."

Ariana nodded and asked, "Do you need me to do anything with this potential hire?"

"You seem better than me with background searches, so if you could do that and suggest a salary, I would appreciate that."

"No, you're better at background searches than me, but I can do a better job than you as far as sensing if she'll get along with your other employees, so that's what I'll check."

They heard the driveway sensors alarm indicating that Hermione was likely home was school. Ariana glanced at the camera just to confirm. She'd had enough people trying to break into her house in the recent couple of years, that it was habit to confirm.

Hermione walked in carrying a backpack and the smell of chlorine on her. "Hi, guys. There's a problem at school that I need your help with, but I've got to shower first," and she disappeared down the hallway.

"Nothing like having a word bomb dropped on us, and then she disappears," Damian said.

"Yep, that's a teenager for you."

The adults worked on dinner while they waited to hear Hermione's school problem. She reappeared in sweats with her short bob mostly dry and the chlorine smell gone.

"So you drop a word bomb on us and then run away before we know anything. What's up with school?" Damian asked.

"One of my classmates went to the office to get a transcript of his grades last week as he's applying to universities in the UK. The office told him then that the system was down, but he would be able to get them soon. Today they still weren't able to supply transcripts, so his parents got involved and the school admitted that someone hacked into the grade system and none of us can get transcripts. That's a problem . . ."

"Because college applications are due by the end of the month in about three weeks," Ariana finished.

"Exactly," Hermione said with a sigh. "My entire senior class is in uproar. I told my friends that Damian could fix the problem and not to worry."

"Ah, I'm glad you have that kind of faith in me, but if a hacker got into the system, they could do serious damage. I think there's a few stories every year of students hacking their school's grading system. How many students are affected by this hack?"

"Just the seniors, apparently. The other classes are fine. You can imagine how anxious everyone is and I would be too, but again, I know that Damian can fix the problem," the teenager said, as though he could throw a switch somewhere and bring all the data back.

"I'll have to contact your school tomorrow and get the full story. Hopefully, I have enough credit with the school that they'll allow me to help."

"My computer science teacher will stick up for you as well as all my coaches."

"The school will be suspicious of me potentially manipulating your grades or perhaps they might think that I am the hacker."

"I was on the honor roll before this happened and the school knows I have straight A's, so there's not much improvement that you can do. You can take me to school in the morning and then go talk to the principal."

Damian was heartened by the confidence that Hermione had in his abilities, but he also thought that it wouldn't be as simple as she thought to convince the school to let him help. He might have to rally Hermione's friends, and other parents he had met at the school.

"I guess I should be honored that you don't mind being seen with your parent on school grounds," he said with a smile.

"Some of my friends think their parents are dorky and out of touch. I don't think that about you, Damian."

"That's backward praise, I think."

"If I were one of my jerky classmates, I'd behave that way, but you two as Parents 2.0 are amazing."

Damian put his hand over his heart and said, "Be still, my beating heart. That's incredible praise from someone your age."

"Yes, well, just save my high school's grading software."

They ate dinner, chatted about other things, and then Hermione retreated to her room to do homework.

"Do you think you can fix Hermione's school problem?" Ariana asked.

"Probably. It will mostly depend on whether the school accepts my help. The powers that be don't know me from Adam. I'm the parent of one of their students, and the last thing they want is for me to make the situation worse. They probably don't know who the hacker is, but they need to worry that it might be me since I'm contacting them and offering to fix it. I'll see how far I can get. It's a good thing we made friends with Hermione's coaches and some of her teachers, as that will give some street cred with the school's administration."

"Imagine if they have to go through the school district process of hiring a consultant to fix it. That will take weeks, and by then the college application deadlines will pass. I'd tell the school to go ahead after their consultant contract, but that you're trying to save every senior student's college application."

"Yeah, I'll try that approach. It's ironic that both the FBI and the SJPD want me on their payroll, but I'll likely have a hard time convincing Hermione's school to take a chance on me."

"Use those agencies as references; that might convince them."

# CHAPTER 3

amian had a restless night as he thought of ways to convince the school to let him help. He also needed to be back across the bay at his warehouse to interview Emily for the marketing position. He decided that he would start out being reasonable with the school, and if that didn't work he would call the FBI on the school to see if they could force him in as an unpaid consultant.

As he had guest-lectured in Hermione's science class, he reached out to that teacher about the problem and his plan. He also asked when the principal usually arrived as there was no point in going to the school if the leadership wasn't there. That teacher had the principal's contact information and was able to set up a meeting on Damian's behalf for eight that morning. He didn't maintain a car at Ariana's house, so she drove him to the school and decided to join him in meeting with the principal. She doubted she would be of any help, but she did know the school better than Damian did.

They arrived at the busy administration office to find many other sets of irate parents. It turned out that Hermione had convinced the other students, who in turn convinced their parents that Damian was the fastest solution to the problem of the missing transcripts. Barraged by angry parents and students, the principal agreed to Ariana's original proposal to hire Damian for free, while they searched for a consultant to fix their problem. He left with a username and password so he could work on the system from his home or from work. He'd been embarrassed by the cheers and clapping of the other parents when they saw the school cooperate and let him try to fix the problem. Hermione must have done quite the sales job on her fellow students.

Ariana dropped him off at her house so he could steer his boat back across the bay. She had meetings of her own to contend with in regard to the start-ups she was funding. Damian made a brief stop at his island to feed his cats and drop off his overnight bag before going on to work. He had about ninety minutes before Emily arrived to think about the questions he wanted to ask her. Ariana had suggested a salary for her; he just needed to ask the right questions to make sure she could do the job and was a fit for his staff.

He put Natalie's case aside for the moment as he had a little more time to handle that compared to the high school transcript problem. He alerted his staff to the school hacking problem, but no one had more expertise in hacking than he did, so they left him to it. He pulled up the system and was getting familiar with the coding.

He was surprised at how fast time had passed when Lily knocked on his doorframe to let him know that Emily had arrived. Time to switch gears. He took a moment to glance at her resume and then chatted with her regarding his company's needs for the Vegas show and then asked her how she would accomplish the tasks. An hour later, he knew Lily's choice was a fit and he made his offer. She accepted and would meet later in the day with Ariana when she had time to stop by and go over the paperwork with her. In the interim he toured her around the warehouse and introduced her to all the staff. Chris and Haley were especially happy to meet her as they both worried about their role at the show. His staff went to lunch with her at Pete's restaurant on the bottom floor, while he made his excuses with needing to dig into the problem with Hermione's school.

Damian operated on the principle that data was never destroyed; it was just hidden in some data trashcan in cyberspace. His first goal was to find the data and save it somewhere for the school. Then he would help them reset their transcript system and take it offline so that the hacker couldn't go after it again. His third duty was to trace the hacker and turn him over to law enforcement.

He was surprised hours later when Ariana knocked on his doorframe to tell him that she liked Emily, and all the paperwork was completed. When he opened his warehouse and hired staff, Ariana had agreed to be his part-time Chief Operating Officer and handle all the human resources issues as she had experience from her start-ups.

"How's the search going for the missing transcripts?"

"I think I'll find them by tonight," Damian said, and then outlined his plan for dealing with the hack.

"As this is the most important thing in your list of priorities, I'll leave you to it and let Hermione know of your timeline when she gets home from practice. I'm sure she'll blast your pending success to everyone and then I'll be fending off phone calls from parents. Good luck," Ariana said, and then with a hug and a kiss she was gone.

Damian looked at the time and decided to wrap up his investigation on the hacker and continue his search for the missing school transcripts. His home computer was as powerful as anything else that he owned. He thought he had a few more walls to go through to find the garbage bin holding the data. The hacker was good, but Damian was better, and he was finding traces of where the data might be. Once he located it, he would transfer it to the cloud and make a few copies for the school on a few external drives so it would be easier to retrieve it the next time a hacker got into the system.

A while later he was home and closing up his dock for the night. He debated fishing for his dinner, but he wasn't in the mood. He wanted to get back on the trail of the hacker as this was one of his favorite computer activities to do. It felt like a competition as to who was the greater computer wizard.

He pulled sandwich stuff out of refrigerator and took his dinner creation and some tea down to his computer lab to continue the search. He was jolted out of his work inside the deep recesses of the dark web by a call from Hermione.

"Hello, Kiddo."

"Ariana said you thought you would recover our transcripts by tonight. Have you found them?"

"I'm close. It's like I'm in a car chase on a curvy road and I can see the hacker's headlights off and on as I chase him."

"Can I come over and watch? I'll stay with you and then leave early to make it to school in the morning. I want to understand what you're doing searching for our grades."

"You might slow me down, Kiddo, if I have to explain what I'm doing. Of course, you're always welcome to spend the night here. So come on over with the understanding that you will slow me down if you have too many questions."

"Yeah!" as all he heard before the line went dead. He looked outside to see if it was dark or light still. If she left immediately, she would navigate the bay in mostly daylight. His system would alarm when she got closer, but as Ariana's boat would have to remain docked outside his watersports garage, he may as well put the dock out now.

He put the dock out and then was startled when the alarm went off, indicating that Hermione was arriving having navigated Ariana's pontoon boat. He left his lab and went outside into the cold and damp air to help the teenager tie down the boat for the night.

They walked inside the lab and Damian said, "Help yourself to any food or drink you want upstairs."

"Ariana made me a big dinner so I'm good. I was planning to sit behind you and see where you're going on the internet."

"Why? This is an area you shouldn't dabble in as everyone is up to no good in this area of the web. I have all kinds of security enhancements to protect me, but the average computer user does not. So don't ever follow me into some of these spaces."

"I want to understand better what you're doing. I'm also going to get a ton of questions from everyone tomorrow if you find the transcripts tonight. I promise not to spend any time without your supervision in this part of the web."

"Good," Damian said. "I'm searching for data by your high school name, as well as your name, your science teacher's name, and another student from your high school. I'm picking up leads on each name—those are the lights I'm seeing on the road of a hacker ahead. I've found your transcript and the transcripts related to classes graded by your science teacher."

"Yeah! At least I can send my application to the university on time," Hermione said, with a big smile. That was the moment Damian realized how worried she was about the missing transcript and her future college acceptance.

"You doubted I would figure this out?" Damian said with a waggle of his eyebrows.

"No. I knew you would figure it out, I just didn't know if you would be able to so by the application deadline which is fast approaching."

"Okay, well let me get back to work on the rest of your class. If I find it tonight, and I think I will, I'll need to follow you back across the bay to school tomorrow. I'm planning on saving the data in the cloud as well as giving your school a flash drive with the data. Then I'll go to work on who was behind the hack."

"I guess I hadn't thought of who was behind the hack, but I suppose that if you find out who, then they'll get arrested as it's illegal to hack into a school, right?"

"Right."

"Not to sound like it's all about me, but I hope it has nothing to do with my parents and me."

Damian hugged her and said, "Kiddo, with all the crap that's been hurdled at you by enemies of your parents, that's not self-centered thinking; it's just preparing yourself if that is the source. Any more questions before I go back to searching? I get in the zone when I'm doing this kind of work, and you might have to shake my shoulder if you see something on fire."

Hermione laughed and said, "I'm going to watch you a bit and then head to my room to do a little homework, answer text inquiries from my classmates, and fall asleep."

She did watch him for a while, but she couldn't understand where he was going on the internet, so she gave up and went to the tiny room he'd made for her off the lab. She made a mental note to herself to ask him to explain when he wasn't in such a hurry. There was a bathroom adjacent to the lab, but if she wanted a shower, she had to go upstairs to his shower. As she was in water polo training, she didn't shower before school this semester.

As she thought, she had texts to answer and homework to do, and she fell asleep listening to the faint click of a keyboard from where Damian was at work.

Damian stood up and stretched just after midnight. He'd finally located where the hacker tried to dispose of the data. He was able to capture it and then he set about saving it to a web, and on two different hard drives—one that he would keep for himself and one for the school. He had a feeling the hacker was not done with the school, and he wanted to save time the next time he went hunting for the data.

He left a note on Hermione's door regarding his success and

went upstairs to sleep. He left an email for the principal about stopping by the next morning. They would have to leave the house by 7 am in order for her to make her first class. He set his alarm and fell into bed puzzling over the hacker's actions. Why would he hack into the school, steal their data, and not request a ransom amount?

The next morning was cold and foggy on San Francisco Bay when Damian and Hermione made their way in their boats across the bay. Ariana had to leave early for meetings in San Jose, so Hermione would take him to her school and then he would get a ride-share back to Ariana's house before going back across the bay to work.

Hermione parked in the student lot and headed toward her classroom. They both passed through security. Damian watched her being stopped by her classmates and he wondered if they were making plans, or if she was giving them updates on their grades.

He followed the route to the principal's office with his spare flash drive in his hand and a temporary visitor badge on his jacket. Damian heard a noise behind him and looked over his shoulder to find a group of students following him. He wondered if they were seniors, and having seen him arrive with Hermione they wanted to find out what he was going to tell the principal? Or maybe their next class was beyond the administration offices and this was the quickest path. He mentally shrugged and continued on to where the principal's assistant sat to announce his presence.

She looked beyond him to the students and said to them, "You'll have to wait out here."

While she went inside to announce his desire to meet with the principal, one of the students behind him asked, "Did you find our transcripts?"

Damian debated his answers and replied, "Probably." It

would take some verification by the school on the accuracy of the grades that he retrieved from the dark web.

The assistant showed him into the office. In addition to the high school principal, he was introduced to the school district's IT expert. For the benefit of the IT expert, Damian explained where he had found the file containing the transcripts. He could tell that the principal had little interest in IT, but was more concerned about what his school would do if the transcripts stayed missing. Now that he knew that Damian had the transcripts stashed in two different places, he relaxed and let the two geeks talk.

Damian showed them where he placed the records in the cloud and on the flash drive. He cautioned against using the school system.

"Why?" ask the principal.

"Your incident is a strange hacking case in that you didn't receive a request for ransom to get the data back. I have another urgent project that requires my attention. Once I'm done with that, I'm going to find your hacker and their motive for doing this hack. For all I know, you may have a brilliant student who took revenge on the school. We need to know about the hacker."

"We can keep the data safe," said the IT person.

"No, you can't. This hacker is good, and they'll figure out how to get into your system again. You have a duty to my senior and all the rest of her class—don't mess with their transcripts just as they're applying to college. That is top of their minds at the moment. Besides, you have work in front of you; you're going to have to verify the data I found as being correct before you start sending it out to colleges. That should be your focus at the moment."

The principal looked impressed with Damian's reasoning. He hadn't expected this computer whiz to suggest that the data he located for their school might be wrong. He put his hand on the IT expert's arm and nodded his agreement.

"You're correct, Mr. Green, with the school's priorities. We will seek to validate the data and prepare ourselves to respond to the college applications. Did you check as to whether Hermione Knowles' grades are correct?"

"I did, only because it was easy. She's had straight A's since she started, and that's what I pulled from the dark web. I also specifically pulled another student and the grades provided by your science teacher. That sampling should allow you to verify that I pulled the correct file."

"Why the science teacher?"

"I know he keeps a separate spreadsheet of every grade he's assigned to students since he began teaching. So you can have him verify the grade of any student who has taken his science class, which is most of the seniors."

"How do you know that?" the principal asked with no inflexion in his voice that might reveal how he felt about Damian knowing that fact about one of his teachers.

"I delivered a guest lecture to his students last year, and he mentioned it. In fact, he said that he expected this school to get hacked someday as it was a TikTok craze, so he was prepared when that happened."

"Oh."

"If you have no more questions, I'll head to work," Damian said, standing up and heading to the door.

"Thank you, Mr. Green. You've handled this situation for us brilliantly. I wasn't in favor of hiring you and went through the process of trying to find a Silicon Valley expert, but the seniors' college aspirations would have been dead by the time I found another expert."

Damian exited the office to find a crowd of students awaiting him. He paused wondering if he should push his way through. Or he could let the Administration office clear a path for him. Then a teary-eyed teen, perhaps a senior, said, "Is it fixed? Can we go to college?"

Damian nodded and was then embarrassed by hordes of random teenagers trying to hug him and give their thanks. Perhaps he should have expected this given the stress he'd seen in Hermione last night. She had an inside track to knowing Damian would likely succeed, whereas these kids had no idea if he was capable of finding their transcripts.

He'd been sure he would find the transcripts, but these kids had lived the past 48 hours worried about whether they could apply to colleges. There were cheers and hugging and Damian was uncomfortable with the gratitude flowing his way. Finally, he hid behind his technical language.

"You all know that nothing ever gets destroyed on the web. I spent hours searching in the dark corners of the web for the trash bin containing your transcripts with a few students' names and a teacher's name. I found the transcripts. They have not been returned to your school system, but your school has a copy on the cloud and on a flash drive. They are verifying that the grades are correct. Keep in touch with the school for the next steps, okay? I need to go to work," he said, trying to get outside so he could call a ride share.

Questions were tossed at him, but he ignored them until one enterprising student said, "I saw that you came with Hermione. Do you need a ride somewhere? I don't have any classes for another half an hour."

"Actually, if someone who doesn't have to skip school could give me a ride to Hermione's house, which is about ten minutes from here, I would appreciate it."

He saw hands raised offering to be his driver and asked, "What are all of you doing here so early at school if you don't have class? Your generation is not known for getting up early."

He got responses that he summed up as: *My future was on the line, I couldn't sleep, I got word that Hermione's guardian found a solution.*

He selected the girl who originally volunteered and said,

"Let's go." He needed to get away from all this teenage emotion. The girl was a friend of Hermione's whom he hadn't met. She was planning on applying to several universities and had been sleepless for days worrying that all her college dreams were dashed. Damian had her let him off at the top of Ariana's driveway and waved her away.

He sighed and headed for the dock, texting Hermione, "I just dealt with a bunch of your classmates. Thanks for not crying on my shoulder over this problem."

As she was in class, Damian didn't expect a reply until he was nearly at his office.

"I had faith you would fix it, but yes, there have been a lot of crying seniors since the transcripts were discovered missing." Damian liked her response and moved on to Natalie's case.

# CHAPTER 4

$\mathcal{A}$s Damian thought about Natalie's case, there were two things at the top of his priority list. What could he find from nearly a decade ago on John Baldwin's movements for the week before his death, and what could he discover to help the widow's case for a bigger share of the IPO?

What data might he find on a skier and frequent visitor to Lake Tahoe? He bet the roads had cameras, the ski resort used RFID tickets, and the casinos were rich with security cameras. Where might he find a depository of such data nearly ten years later? Damian was a computer hacker who was far better than the one that attacked Hermione's school. He relished the chance to hack into the casino security system as he'd bet that theirs was one of the most sophisticated software systems around. He smiled and rubbed his fingers together at the challenge ahead.

He startled when someone knocked on his door. It was Emily, and he had an appointment with her that he'd completely forgotten about.

"Sorry, we had an appointment scheduled, but you look like you just discovered the Theory of Relativity or something like that breakthrough. That would be the limit of my geek speak, by the way."

He laughed and said, "Yeah, there's a lot of geek speak here. At least we follow sports, so there's a common language there. Have a seat."

Emily smiled, sat down and replied, "Yes, I have common ground with sports talk, restaurant menus, and beer as I've discovered speaking with the rest of the staff here."

"Good, then you know everything about everyone now. Did Haley and Chris demonstrate the technologies we'll be sharing at the CES show?"

"Yes, and I've got ideas. I wanted to understand your desired endgame from the show. I haven't attended the CES show, but I watched old videos on it. I thought the thing we should decide first is who is your desired audience?"

"Rather than answer your question, let me describe the desired outcome of the show—I would like the technologies we display to have an offer for production that includes royalty payments to this company."

"Do you want two marketing strategies, then? Perhaps one directed at investors and another directed at the public that explains your products?"

"I'm not looking for an investor; I'm looking for a company that wants to produce our products. An investor is a middleman that I don't need. We don't need funding to develop products; rather, they are at the completed stage and we're looking for a manufacturing plant to turn our specifications over to so they can make and sell the product."

"Got it. I'll employ two strategies: one to gather the attention of news organizations as your manufacturer might not be at the show, but they might catch news of the show; and a second focus that describes a manufacturing process so that someone walking by would say, 'yes, I can add that to my assembly line.'"

"Perfect. We're all here to help you with that to the degree we can help," Damian said, then added. "Do you have any other questions I can answer?" He was anxious to get back to trying to hack into a casino and was relishing the opportunity to do so.

"No. I also wanted to thank you for hiring me and providing health insurance even though I'm a short-term employee. You've made preparing for this baby a whole lot easier."

"It's a two-way street. I needed someone with your talents for the CES show, but I didn't have permanent work for you to do. I thought I would end up contracting with a company to provide that sort of short-term intense work. You're a much better solution as you're our employee, not some nameless company's employee."

Emily departed soon after and Damian decided to grab lunch from Pete's restaurant before going back to work. He texted his order and they would text him when it was ready. They would willingly deliver it, but he was strict on his security, and no one came inside the building without his doing a deep dive into their background.

While he was waiting for the text, he checked in with Hermione's school to see if they had verified the student transcript files. The hacker was either lazy or arrogant. Either they were too lazy to really mess up the grades by randomly changing them or they arrogantly thought that no one had the hacking skills to find out where they stashed the data and therefore could leave it in its original form. The school verified the grades against the science teacher's spreadsheet and there were no discrepancies. They planned to tell the students that to the best of their knowledge the grades were correct, and they should verify them and provide proof if they were wrong. Damian replied to the school that he had looked at the coding behind the transcripts and the last entry was before the hack occurred, so he was sure the hacker hadn't tampered with the original grades.

His text arrived and he skipped down to the restaurant to

pick up his food. Pete had his staff provide Damian and his team with foil-wrapped plates and real silverware knowing that they would be returned to his restaurant after their meals were consumed.

He'd forgotten to eat breakfast and was tearing into a juicy cheeseburger and fries. Some days just called for that kind of meal. While he ate, he thought about where he should look for cameras in the Lake Tahoe region. His biggest problem was a lot of those cameras had little to no storage and were likely written over so many times that any original video would be difficult to watch. According to the police report, the family's Tahoe residence was in the city of South Lake Tahoe. There were many casinos in that area just over the Nevada boundary in the city of Stateline. There were also casinos in Incline Village and Crystal Bay, but they were nearly an hour's drive and they were small casinos. That left Damian with a handful of Stateline casinos to hack into. Fortunately, the two largest were owned by a single company and he would start there.

Before he knew it, his lunch was devoured, and he found his first back door into the casinos. By state law they only needed to save their recordings for six months, but most of them saved the tapes for years as they were used to identify card cheaters.

Damian began worming his way through their security system. He was grateful that these two casinos had upgraded to digital cameras before John Baldwin died. He would have had a fairly worthless search if the cameras were analog. He kept digging deeper to find the recordings for the month of John's death. He looked up at the time, startled to see that it was dark outside and apparently all his staff had already left for the night. He took a deep breath, stretched to clear his head, and tried to remember if any of them had said goodnight and if he'd responded. He decided that he had waved them off while staring at his computer screen. His staff would know he was lost in the depths of the internet and would barely respond to outside stimuli.

The clock said seven, so it was time to head home and pay attention to the rest of the world. Soon he was locking up his office door and he smiled as he looked at the restaurant. He was an investor in Pete's second location, and he was happy to see that the parking lot was busy. Pete had scouted the neighborhood before he built the restaurant, and it was nice to see his intel bear out.

He was at the marina in no time and then in his small boat heading for home. He hit the remote to open the door to his watercraft garage, and then a dock folded out. In no time he had his watercraft tucked away and the island closed up for the night. He went upstairs to a chorus of meows from Bailey and Bella. He'd left them inside and it had been an especially long day. They wanted their supper and then would head outside to hunt for the night.

He took care of his cats, grabbed a small meal himself, and then settled back in his lab to do some work. While he enjoyed tracking down data and playing in other people's information systems, his eyes were tired. He had spent hours the previous day searching for Hermione's classmates' transcripts and now he using facial recognition to search for evidence of where John Baldwin was before his unfortunate death.

He knew he needed to give his brain and his body a break, so he turned on a basketball game featuring his favored Golden State Warriors. He watched it for a short time and then felt himself drifting off to sleep. He shook himself awake, stood up, turned the game off, and minutes later was sound asleep in bed.

Sometimes his brain worked while he was asleep and he woke up with great ideas; other times there was nothing, or at least nothing that he could remember. Sadly, this morning was not one of those productive nights. He sighed and thought about the day ahead. What could he do for Sara Baldwin to help her court case? He had about three weeks to find proof of her husband's impact on the company. She had a court case scheduled for a month away, but Damian was sure she was being pressured into a settlement. He wanted to get word to her not to settle so he could have time to find answers.

He pulled out one of his burner phones that bounced all over the world. He texted the widow with the message, "I am searching for proof of your husband's impact on the company, but I need time. Try to avoid accepting an out-of-court settlement up to the day before your court case. I will text you any proof of evidence I find. Good luck to you and me."

He supposed it was rather a creepy message and perhaps he should have met her first with Natalie by his side, but it wouldn't hurt her situation, creepy message or not.

Damian reread his message several times and then hit the send button. She wouldn't be able to communicate back to him, but maybe it would make her feel better to know that someone was on her side.

Then he did his usual morning routine and was ready to leave his island for his warehouse. He could have just worked from home, but with a new employee and other questions his staff might have about their work, it was best to go into the office. Sometimes his staff helped him with his cold cases by providing a different perspective.

He'd hired Lily after such a research question. He'd asked Angus if he knew any bank robbers and after he was done laughing at Damian's request, he'd introduced him to Lily who had served time for bank robbery, but who also had a degree in mathematics. Her parole required that she have a paying job, but she'd become independently wealthy with her stock market strategies. Since she was now raising a son, she planned to never do any additional criminal activity, so she was a safe hire for Damian. In addition, Damian had threatened her that if she ever felt an itch to try bank robbery again, he would hack into her investments and destroy all of her wealth.

He walked into the office and asked his staff for a few minutes of their time. He explained the case of John Baldwin, and what was going on now. Then he asked for angles he might research. The first suggestions were what he'd already thought of, but he didn't want to tell them that. He just wanted to keep the flow of suggestions going.

"Did you look at his bank transactions? I would have thought the police looked into that at the time, but maybe they just gave it a superficial review," Lily suggested.

"I haven't gone there yet, thanks for the suggestion."

"How about his data? Have you hacked into the company email to find a trail of his work?" Chris said.

"Since this company was a start-up, I bet there are some early investor presentations that he took part in if he was the engineering brains of the outfit," Haley said.

Damian nodded. The last suggestion he would discuss with Ariana as she was heavily involved in the start-up world and would know where some ancient presentations were kept. He bet that some of the venture capital companies had long records of what presentations they listened to each week. Maybe he could find one of those that demonstrated John Baldwin's contribution to the company.

"Thanks for the suggestions. I know sleuthing isn't what we produce in this company, but I'm hoping to help a widow who is running out of time to claim her proceeds from an IPO. I'll work with Ariana to investigate any PowerPoint presentation decks from almost a decade ago that would demonstrate the dead engineer's contribution to the company."

"I like to help my mother-in-law in a unique way, so keep asking us questions. Besides, serving justice to the family of the tech engineer aligns with this company's values of making the world a better place," Haley said. Natalie Severino was her husband's mother, and she really liked the retired detective.

Damian smiled at Haley's response and thought it likely that she spoke for her co-workers, too. The company's first licensed inventions, for which they were all earning royalties, brought solar-powered electricity from ocean wave action to remote areas of the globe. Their device had eliminated the cost of oil and reduced greenhouse gas emissions. Most of all, people weren't living lives in the dark. Most of the work they did in Damian's company was for the greater good of humanity.

With a few more ideas to pursue for the cold case and the fact that none of his employees needed his help with what they were working on, he was left to retreat to his office and chase some of the suggestions of his employees. He started by looking for a presentation by Baldwin's company. He looked at the venture capital firms located in Palo Alto and wondered if he knew anyone working at any of them. The firms tended to have mobile partners, and then those partners would spin off and create new firms. It could be a convoluted maze watching how people moved from firm to firm.

He gave up after half an hour and instead did a search for Sunnyside AI with the time period of six months before the skier's death. There was evidence that the company was doing many presentations in the lead-up to their eventual funding by one of the major venture capital firms. There were records of presentations by John Baldwin and the current CEO. These recordings confirmed for Damian that John was the brain of the company. There had been questions asked that the current CEO couldn't answer despite his trying to hog the spotlight in any presentation.

After watching a few presentations, he decided they really need to speak to Sara Baldwin. He bet that she knew what was going on with the company during this time period. He picked up the phone to call Natalie.

"Hey, what have you found?" she asked after they finished their greetings.

"Did you know that your victim's widow has been tied up in a court case for the past three years?"

"No. What's the case about?"

"She's suing Grape AI, which is the new name for Sunnyside AI. She feels that she should have received proceeds from the IPO from her former husband's company as it was his coding that created the system. The IPO would have generated millions, and from what I can see she is correct. However, she doesn't have enough proof yet and time is running out. Sara is my first priority at the moment. Can you set up an interview with her for you and me?" Damian asked, giving Natalie his availability.

"Yes. I'll ask her about her husband's movements and then you can ask her about the court case. It would be a nice win to solve the murder and get money for the guy's widow. Did she get any money at the time of his death?"

"The company wasn't making any money yet and they were still doing presentations trying to get private equity funding. So near as I can tell, she just got a life insurance payout."

"Okay, we probably looked at that at the time of the guy's death to cross her off as a murderer even though we never declared the case a homicide. I'll read the detective notes before we visit her. How much is she suing the company for?"

"Fifty million. That's about 10 percent of its net worth. I would say that is not an unreasonable amount based on what the CEO has earned over the decade."

"Wow. That's not chump change. Can you lay out a diagram for me about the company? That would also help me understand who John's enemies might be if it becomes a homicide."

"You want an organization chart?" Damian asked, puzzled.

"No. Can you tell me where the company started and where it is now?"

"Ah yes, of course."

They ended their call shortly thereafter and Damian got to work on the diagram for Natalie. It was also good for him to understand the situation for John's widow. He researched some milestones that the company made and what John Baldwin's contributions had been to the company. He sent it off to Natalie and realized his workday was at an end. Again, nearly an entire day passed with his not feeling the passage of time. He enjoyed deep diving into computer systems and understanding the path of a company.

He was headed to Ariana's for dinner and a conversation about start-ups. He'd texted her an update on the case. He was anxious to know if she knew of any places he could look for the historical contribution of John Baldwin. He arrived at her house and after a hug and kiss, he took Miguel outside for an exhausting game of fetch. They retreated inside after the dog had gulped water from his bowl outside on the deck. He flopped down in the living room as Damian took a seat at Ariana's kitchen island.

"That smells great. What are you cooking?"

She pulled a food container out of the trash and said, "I'm making lasagna from scratch as you can see."

"Ah, I remember back to one of our first meetings when you told me you would likely try to impress me with your cooking skill by doing exactly this. It's been a while since you resorted to that cooking strategy."

"I had a desire for lasagna today, but not the time to make it from scratch, so I put an order in at lunchtime with Giuseppe's and picked it up on the way home. I will cook the salad from scratch."

"Cook the salad? I'm envisioning wilted and soggy lettuce among other ingredients."

"Well, I'm cooking the salad, just not with heat."

Damian chuckled over her definition of cooking. Then Ariana completely switched gears.

"There's a repository of start-up presentation decks at the Museum of Technology. The repository is not online, but you can search it in person. You can do searches in a variety of ways including by your victim's name. Not all of the venture capital firms contribute to it, but the vast majority do for reasons of intellectual property and for historical value. Many young guns in Silicon Valley think they've invented the wheel for the first time, but any wise VC firm reviews the presentation deck against those in the past. Getting into a fight over intellectual property can sink a company before it has made its first dime."

"I'll head there tomorrow. I didn't know they had such a thing, and I'm surprised that it's not online."

"I think the creators feared someone hacking into the repository and changing the decks. Besides many of the presentations have written notes on the pages about what is wrong about the concept, and that is amazing as well. I have a meeting in San Jose tomorrow morning and if you want to move your boat to a harbor close by the museum, I can give you a ride the rest of the way to the museum. That way you can head home or to work after you're done."

"I asked Natalie to set up a meeting with Sara Baldwin as I wanted to ask her questions about her husband's role and let her know I was joining her fight. Natalie can more easily do that under the guise of reopening the case of her husband's death. Hopefully that will be set up for tomorrow, and I can kill two errands to Silicon Valley in one boat ride."

Ariana's security system beeped and when she looked at it, she could see Hermione's car moving down the driveway. Damian began setting the table and the teenager walked inside the house.

"What's for dinner? It smells great!" she asked, getting a hug from Ariana and then Damian.

"It's lasagna. Are you hungry?"

"I am. Water polo practice was a series of swimming sprints and goal drills. We didn't practice our usual game workout, so it was harder. By the way, Damian, the entire senior class thinks you're dope."

"That's good, right?"

Hermione shook her head in exasperation. Damian knew that being called "dope" was high praise, but he wanted to yank her chain.

"Was everyone able to verify their grades as correct?"

"Yes. A few students tried to argue for higher grades, but they targeted the wrong teachers. It turns out that other teachers besides the science teacher were also keeping spreadsheets, and they were all proven wrong. Once word got out about that, no one else challenged the grades. I heard that the hacker tried to get into our system again, but failed as the IT guy sensed it and blocked it."

"That's concerning. I wonder why the hacker came back for a second attack? I'd planned to look into them, but I'm working on another ticking-clock assignment, so I can't get to that for a few days, but I will research it. Your class is safe as far as college applications go, isn't it?"

"Yes. The principal said that you gave him a copy of the transcripts that is not connected to the internet and that's what they're using to send our grades out to universities. The problem is that in the past it was automated, but this is manual, so it's taking more clerical time. Several parents volunteered to give the school money to pay for outside clerical help. So we should be good."

"I didn't think of the practicalities of responding to universities. I can imagine that they had a fairly slick system for sending transcripts. If I had time, I could create something for the school to use, but I don't have time at the moment. So I think the solution created by the other parents is great. If they need more funds, let us know; we can contribute to the fund."

"I don't think they would allow you to contribute. You're the school hero who saved my graduating class's college aspirations. I think most of the parents are wealthy, so there is plenty of money from them to get the transcripts released to the universities," Hermione said.

Damian had to agree with Hermione's comment about the other parents—the average home price in this area was over four million dollars. Hermione was right, and he changed his mind on the offer to help on this problem.

"What else is going on at school? Are you guys gossiping about who the hacker is?"

"We did gossip, but we don't think any of the best computer science kids could be our hacker. So we students have decided it's an outside source."

That caught Damian's attention. He couldn't help but wonder if this was an enemy of his ward's real parents. They had tried kidnapping her several times. They had sent her social media posts trying to trick her into meetings. They wanted Hermione to use as leverage against her parents. Perhaps their latest tactic is if they couldn't kidnap her, then they would try and negatively affect her future. It wouldn't serve as leverage with her parents, but it might feel like a satisfying piece of revenge. He filed those thoughts away until he could do something about the hacker. In the interim, Hermione's college future and that of her classmates was safe. It was a reminder to Damian that he couldn't let his guard down around Hermione until all of the court cases that her parents were involved in were resolved.

After dinner they played a short game of Fortnite before Hermione retreated to her room to study. Damian and Ariana took a blanket and a bottle of wine outside to sit on the deck and enjoy the clear night sky. So often there was fog around the bay at night that one couldn't see the stars but tonight was an exception. They discussed their business issues as well as the next vacation to plan and then retired for the night.

# CHAPTER 6

Damian left the house an hour before Ariana. Despite the traffic, a boat could only go so fast—about a third of the speed of her car. Plus, he needed to spend time docking his boat, paying the fee and walking out of the harbor to Ariana's car. On his way south, Natalie texted him with an appointment to meet with Sara Baldwin around noon. Natalie would pick Damian up from the museum and drop him back to the harbor.

The museum was surprisingly fascinating. It had some presentation decks from when some large companies had just been a glimmer in their founder's eye. He had to ignore his interest in those companies that had become unicorns as they were known for being valued at over one billion dollars and continue to search for Sunnyside AI. He found several decks and made copies of them to look at later. He was running out of time as Natalie would pick him up soon. He hadn't researched Sara Baldwin's background to be able to guess the degree that she understood her late husband's work at the start-up. He thought a few of the presentations would prove that her husband had had a big role in the invention.

He met Natalie in front of the museum and they drove to an average neighborhood in south San Jose. It was a housing tract in which every sixth or eighth house was the same. If she won her court case, Damian guessed she would be moving elsewhere. Natalie knocked on the door and showed her badge to the woman who answered it, who identified herself as Sara Baldwin, and after they were invited inside, she introduced Damian.

Natalie explained about the reopening of the cold case concerning her husband's death and began asking questions. "How often during that time period did your husband head to Lake Tahoe?"

Sara smiled with the memory, "John was always a ski bum. He liked to say that he held a job to take care of his family and to ski. During most ski seasons, he would go up to Lake Tahoe at least every other weekend and sometimes he would stay for the week."

"Do you ski?"

"I did until we had children, but I was never at his ability level, and we would often go our own ways once we reached a resort. I like the intermediate slopes, and I would occasionally try an advanced run. He liked to jump off bowl ridges. He could have starred in a Warren Miller film. It was why I stopped skiing when we had kids, as I was sure he was going to kill himself on a steep slope one day. In the end, he did die on skis, but not where anyone would have thought he would die. He would be horrified to know he died in a flat park wearing cross-country skis."

"So he didn't use cross-country skis?" Damian asked.

"No. There was no thrill with cross country. He had those types of skis, but it was only for a cardio workout if he used the skis to run errands. There was no reason for John to be at the Emerald Bay State Park as there were no grocery stores or restaurants. Also, he was staying at a condo in Stateline. That would have been about perhaps twelve miles each way at dusk. I've always been sure he was murdered as nothing about the scene of his death makes sense."

"Mrs. Baldwin, I know you've been asked many questions about your husband at the time of his death but bear with me as I likely repeat some of those questions. Did John or you receive any threats from any source prior to his passing?"

Sara paused to think about the question and answered, "No. John didn't seem any more stressed than he usually was. He spent hours coding the technology for the company and attending presentations to try to get funding for their start-up. He often said that skiing allowed his brain to develop solutions to problems he saw in the software."

"Do you remember the names of any of the venture capital companies that he did presentations of the technology to?" Damian asked.

"No. Why?"

Damian paused, thinking about his answers, and then replied, "I'm aware of the lawsuit you have against your husband's company to gain his share of the IPO proceeds. I want to help and I'm probably uniquely positioned to do that. I actually sent you a text from a burner phone, but you probably thought it was from random creep."

Sara looked at him confused. "I thought you were with the police. What's this about?"

"I am assisting the police. I've helped on several cold cases as I'm a computer geek and can crunch large amounts of data to find answers. When Natalie asked for my help with this case, it was with the intent of determining what killed your husband. I, of course, investigated you and discovered the lawsuit. I want to help you get your husband's share of the company he helped to create. I'm an unpaid consultant to the San Jose Police Department. I'm looking into your case to see what evidence I can find to assist you."

All of a sudden, big tears ran down Sara's face. Natalie moved next to the woman and ran a hand down her back as they waited for her to regain her composure. Damian waited for Sara's next statement as he couldn't tell what the tears meant.

Finally she said, "I've been on this journey all by myself for several years. Other than my attorney, no one has offered to help me, and frankly, my attorney is after his cut if we win, but he doesn't care about the fairness of this situation. John worked one-hundred-hour weeks in the months before his death. He would code from Lake Tahoe. We were scrimping to afford everything because you don't get paid much with a start-up. His partners were marketing people and hadn't a clue about coding. So for John to do all the technology work of the company and for them to refuse to share proceeds of the IPO with John's family is theft."

"I was just at the Technology Museum this morning looking for early presentations he did. Many venture capital firms send their PowerPoint decks to the museum. I found three decks that show coding progress that should be useful in your court case. Did your attorney hire an IT expert to assist with uncovering evidence for this case?" Damian asked.

"No."

"You should fire him or her, as that is malpractice."

"He said that as John's wife I was the expert, but my training isn't in start-ups or coding. I'd love to fire him, but when I tried he pointed to the contract I signed with his firm."

"I know an Intellectual Property attorney. How about if I set up a meeting for today or tomorrow and he evaluates whether you can fire your current attorney based on legal malpractice? I have IP myself and he is my IP attorney. He'll look at your case as a favor to me."

Her eyes watered again, and she nodded.

"Natalie, why don't you ask Mrs. Baldwin your questions and I'll make the call to my attorney," Damian said, standing up and exiting the room to make the call. He came back a short time later, and said, "Marcus is booked up the rest of the day, but he can meet us for dinner. Are you available, Sara?"

"I usually have dinner with my kids, but they're old enough to be on their own. Tell me when and where and I'll be there."

Damian supplied her with the name of a restaurant and time, then he moved on to more questions.

"Did your husband save any work on a home computer or leave any papers in a home office?"

"Yes. I've had an old desktop tower sitting in my garage that John used. I'm appalled I didn't think of it earlier or my attorney didn't ask that question. Just a moment and I'll go fetch what I have."

After she left the room, Damian looked at Natalie and shook his head. "This situation makes me so mad. It's bad enough she lost her husband, but then his company screws his widow, and she has a bad attorney on top of it. I think I'll look into the attorney. He is awfully suspicious."

Sara returned carrying a black tower which she put on the floor in front of Damian. Then she said, "There's a box I need to bring inside; just a moment."

"Do you need help?" Damian said to her retreating back.

"No, thank you. Be back in a sec."

She returned carrying a box labeled with "John Work Stuff" and placed that at Damian's feet. He was itching to get onto the computer to see what was saved there versus what the finished product looked like for the company. They asked a few more questions about John's habits and then left the house. Damian would see Sara later that evening and keep Natalie informed about what he found on the computer and in the box.

Natalie was about to drop him off at the marina when he thought of one more question, "Did you get his cellphone records at the time of his death? Also, I forgot to ask where John's laptop was for the work he did remotely. I'm sure he took one with him to Lake Tahoe. I'll ask Sara about that tonight, but was there a record of what was in his condo at the time of his death?"

"Let me look at what the El Dorado County folks recorded as they would have been the ones to go to the condo, but since his death was not defined as a homicide, we may not have cell-phone records or condo contents from the date of his death," Natalie said, and they said their goodbyes.

Damian thought about the case on his way back across the bay to his island. He wasn't a detective, but there were so many strange circumstances with this case that he had to think that it would eventually be labeled as a homicide. He also wanted to research Sara Baldwin's attorney. It felt like he didn't do any basic discovery of evidence for the court case.

He reached the island and made Bella and Bailey a fresh fish meal as they had had to survive on their kibble for almost twenty-four hours. He checked in with his office and there were no burning questions for him there and so he went to work on the computer that Sara had given him. It was an old desktop and when he turned it on, he needed to avoid an automatic soft-ware update and fortunately he knew how to do that. He found a treasure trove of all the coding that John did through the months to perfect their product. The evidence was all on the desktop.

Next he began his search on Sara's attorney. Damian could tell by his actions the man was unqualified for any kind of case involving intellectual property. He couldn't find any informa-tion about him practicing in the area of intellectual property or patents. In fact, he couldn't find any California Bar information on the man. Maybe his attorney would be better at finding information on the man. He would have to ask Sara this evening where she found the man. He moved on to the box of papers and again found a wealth of evidence for Sara's case. John had kept several presentations with notes on them of coding changes he would make.

Damian summarized what he found for his dinner discussion and then got ready to boat back across the bay. He would need to take a ride-share service to the restaurant from a marina he found that had an available boat slip. He could have taken his boat to Richmond and driven to the restaurant, but for most of the day it was faster to boat than to drive as traffic was so bad.

He arrived early to the restaurant and checked in with Ariana. She was thrilled that it seemed like he would be able to help Sara Baldwin. He ended the call as he saw his attorney approach and Sara wasn't far behind him. He stood to make introductions.

"Sara Baldwin meet Marcus Blackstone." They shook hands and were shortly seated at a quiet table. Damian got right to business by handing each of them the notes he made on examination of the computer and box.

"My life would be so much easier if you would let my firm hire you as an expert witness. This is excellent work, and I can absolutely see a case here for proceeds from the IPO. Sara, tell me what your current attorney has done for you," Marcus said.

"The IPO was a couple of years ago. I contacted John's old partner at the firm and asked if John's estate would receive any of the proceeds. At the time of John's death, I was working as a nurse and in fact I still am. John had a life insurance policy and that went to pay down the mortgage, and the boys and I could live on my salary. It's been a struggle and some of the IPO proceeds only seemed fair given John's work on the case. His partner, Ryan Alexander, told me that they had hired a new engineer after John's death and the original work created by my husband was not used for the final product as he wasn't around to code. However, from every description I saw of the company, it sounded exactly like what John created. Then I got a call from an attorney. His name is Felix Harris. He said he heard about my problem with Grape AI, which is the new name for Sunnyside AI, which was the name of the company when my husband worked there. So I met with him and discussed my case. I signed a letter of engagement and best of all, I didn't have to pay up front as he would take a contingency fee as a part of the proceeds."

While Sara was talking, Marcus was scrolling on his phone and frowning.

Sara broke off when she noticed the attorney's inattention.

"Sara, there is a court case filed against Grape AI, but you're listed as the attorney of record. I don't see a note of a Felix Harris. I also can't find a Felix Harris in the California State Bar. Has the court corresponded with you?" Marcus asked.

"What? He told me he had filed the paperwork. I don't understand."

"Someone filed paperwork on your behalf as your signature is on the court filing. However, at this time you do not have an attorney representing you and you're about to have the case thrown out of court as you've had two years to submit evidence, and you haven't done so."

Sara put her hands to her face at this latest betrayal by John's former partner. She was sure that he had orchestrated the fake attorney and court case. She felt like shedding more tears, but instead she sighed and looked at the two men dining with her.

"What do I do now?"

"If you would like, I can be your attorney and file suit on your behalf. With this summary provided by Damian, I can likely take care of this tomorrow. You will need to sign a letter of engagement, and we need to agree to the amount you're asking for. I'll need you to stop by my office tomorrow and sign those documents. I'll also need to notify the clerk about the other lawsuit and the falsification of your signature. I will also recommend that Felix Harris be charged with criminal fraud for impersonating an attorney. With your permission I'll report him to the District Attorney, and they may reach out to you."

"I feel like such an idiot for not looking into this situation more. I should have known something was up when Felix stopped returning my phone calls a month ago."

"The good news is we have time to fix it, and if this Felix Harris is linked to Ryan Alexander, then I suspect your IPO proceeds will increase," Marcus said with a fierce smile.

She nodded, then added, "I can't thank you enough for looking at my situation. With your help, my future and that of my children will be secured. Mr. Green, if you're as successful at my husband's cold case as you are with this lawsuit, I think I'll finally have answers as to what happened to John."

"Yes, I'm working on that, but I wanted to intervene with your court case as it looked to me that a terrible wrong was being done to you and your family. With Marcus's help, you'll quickly be on the right track. I'm also going to look into Felix Harris. I suspect that is not his real name, but I have software that may identify him, so I'll assist Marcus with part of the case, too."

While they were talking, they were eating their dinner and Sara could tell that both men were anxious to dig into her case and move forward. She couldn't wait to hear how Ryan Alexander responded to the new lawsuit with a real attorney. She would love to be a fly on the wall when he was notified.

# CHAPTER 7

*D*amian was backing away from the dock where he'd left his boat to meet Marcus and Sara for dinner. It was a foggy night with limited visibility. He kept alert looking for boats and ferries, but mostly for other small crafts like his. Smaller boats often didn't use the AIS system which would show their boats on a screen. The wind was quiet that night and he hoped he would hear a boat before he saw it. Then again, maybe given the level of fog, most boaters would stay home.

He made it to his island without incident and never got close enough to see another boat through the fog. He was thinking about Sara's fake lawyer and was now more than ever convinced that her husband's death was a homicide. A CEO who would go to the trouble of creating a fake lawyer would likewise hire someone to murder his partner or maybe even do it himself. The question was, "How did he accomplish it?"

He sent a text to Natalie about the fake lawyer and the steps they were taking to improve the situation for Sara. He reiterated his request for cell phone records from a decade ago. He thought it likely that they would come up with records, but it would take a few days. He then wanted to run down Felix

Harris. When he looked him up earlier it was the thought that he was a real attorney, but now he wanted a picture of the guy so he could help get him prosecuted for impersonating a lawyer. He texted Sara to find out where and when she first met with Felix. That would tell him if he could find him on a camera somewhere and then capture his image for identification.

With all the fresh air from zooming across the bay that day, he fed the cats and himself and settled into an earlier sleep. His brain was exhausted, and next week Hermione was to begin her water polo matches, and he would try to make all of them. He recorded the games and sent them to her parents and to the coach. The coach used them much like an NFL team did film study—it was easy for the players to see their mistakes. He thought about how he and Marcus had turned the situation around for Sara, and likely Marcus would make a huge financial difference in her life. He felt very satisfied with his work on behalf of Hermione's school, Sara's case, and his firm's readiness for the Computer Electronic Show. There was more work on all those issues, but he had made substantial progress for each problem, he thought as he drifted off to sleep.

The next morning he was in the office before anyone else. That was in part to make up for his absence the previous day. Today was the day he met with all the staff, and they reviewed their progress on their projects. However, that wasn't for hours yet which meant that he could follow up on his search for Felix Harris. Sara had returned his text with the location of their meetings. She never met his at "his office"; instead, they would meet for a meal or a coffee. She looked through her paperwork, but did not have a business card for him. She wanted to kick herself for not doing due diligence on Felix Harris, but he had come along when she didn't know what she was going to do next. Regardless, Damian had a few locations to check out for video cameras. He would search for Sara and see if any man was talking to her or shaking hands in view of a camera. His biggest problem was that the meetings were up to two years ago and most street cameras didn't keep footage that long.

He also did a search for Felix Harris, but there were several people by that name, and he thought it was an alias anyway. Then he had an idea; he would search for Ryan Alexander and Felix Harris together to see if he got any hits. There was a hit, and while it didn't give him a lot of information it indicated a relationship. Felix Harris was a classmate of Ryan Alexander at university. However, it appeared the real Felix Harris died shortly after they graduated from college. This told him that Felix Harris was related to Ryan Alexander and that it was likely an alias. That was a mistake picking a fake name of your fake lawyer that was the same as a college buddy.

Damian passed that piece of information onto Natalie. The more he dug into the case, the more likely he thought that Ryan Alexander might have had something to do with John Baldwin's death. The question was how.

He heard noises out in the warehouse and realized the others were gathering for their weekly meeting. He better head out there and focus on work. Damian spent the next two hours problem solving with his staff. It was a nice brain break from Sara Baldwin's troubles. He looked at the clock and thought that by now Marcus might have filed the paperwork for the case. Normally, the lawyer would lose time gathering material for a court case, but Damian's notes and collection of evidence had greatly sped up that process, allowing the attorney to file the case and spend a few weeks gathering additional evidence to what was already provided by Damian.

He was most interested to see what Ryan Alexander's next step would be. Damian could sit on the sidelines of the case, not revealing his identity, but watching this chump be stuck paying Sara for the work her husband did before he died. He was disappointed in Ryan. He and his three start-up employees made a boat load of money from the IPO, and it would have been easy to give Sara, say, ten million dollars and she would have likely been satisfied with that as it would give her and her boys a financial cushion. Instead, the man had hoarded more money than he could likely spend in his lifetime.

He started his search for images of the man purported to be Felix Harris. They were fortunately near an intersection that had cameras for red light traffic tickets. Damian hacked into the city works department to look for the date of Sara's meeting with Felix. After two hours of searching, he thought he found his image. However, the picture was too pixelated for him to use his facial recognition software to identify him. Nonetheless, he watched him walk to a car and drive off. Damian focused on the license plate and wrote down the combination of letters and numbers. He asked Natalie to run the plate for him explaining who he thought he was.

As Natalie was a retired detective she had to reach out to someone else to run the plates for her, which took time; however eventually she texted that the owner of the car was Fabio Hursa, a local actor in community theatre. He found a driver's license picture of the man and forwarded it to Sara for her to confirm that it was the man she knew as Felix Harris.

She replied back quickly confirming his identity. She also heaped thanks on Damian for his help and mentioned that her meeting with Marcus went well. Damian moved on to find a connection between Ryan Alexander and Fabio Hursa. He put their two pictures together and searched for an image of when the two were physically together, and bingo, he found two instances where they were face to face. He forwarded that information to Natalie and to Marcus. He could send it to his contact at the District Attorney's office and they could bring Fabio in for questioning.

His phone rang and he could see it was Natalie. "Hi. What's up?"

"When I took on this cold case, I never saw the angles you've uncovered so far. The fake attorney and its connection to John Baldwin's co-founder is just too coincidental to ignore. I know you looked into the court case out of a sense of justice for his widow, but wow, it reflects on John's death. Any thoughts on the murder weapon since you've had a run of brilliance so far on this case?"

"I'm not by any means an expert on murder weapons, but I would look at something that leaves little trace like some poisons. Could he have met someone for dinner and they put something in his drink, or could he have been gassed by a deadly agent? I think we need cell phone records to help with that. You need to speak with a physician—perhaps a medical examiner about possible agents, but here's the thing: Even if you declare him a homicide, that doesn't get you closer to finding his killer."

"True that. I've heard of a woman whom the department had interacted with on occasion. She's a retired forensic pathologist. Let me see if I can bring her in on this case, or at least have a conversation with her about the possibilities. You're working the Ryan Alexander angle?"

"I am. I don't like how he treated his partner's widow, and while I would be very surprised that a tech CEO would be at the center of this death, I'm wondering what other things happened in his past life. The fact that his best friend died shortly after they finished college makes me suspicious. The fact that he named a fake lawyer after that friend is weird. I'm going to look into what happened there. Maybe there's a pattern."

"This case is far more complex than I expected. There are these additional angles related to the company that were not apparent at the time of John Baldwin's death. I'll have to update my LT about these latest angles and the fact that his death will likely become a homicide," Natalie said.

"Let me know what your forensic pathologist says about

potential causes of death as that might make me think of new avenues to explore."

"Will do."

Damian ended the call and sat quietly at his desk, but couldn't think of anything to add to the John Baldwin case. He needed additional information from Natalie. It was time to change directions and start searching for Hermione's school hacker. He wanted to know the reason for the hack as he didn't think her high school was randomly chosen.

He was deeply buried in a dark corner of the web searching for the hacker when his phone rang with an unrecognized number. He let it go to voicemail and then read the message after it was transcribed. The call piqued his interest and he punched his telephone keys to return the call.

"This is Dr. Jill Quint. Is this Damian Green?"

"Yes."

"I was calling to chat about the death of John Baldwin, but I have a friend who is very interested in meeting you."

"I didn't know you knew of me before this call."

"I think we have both interacted with FBI Special Agent Leticia Ortiz. She's referenced you as giving my IT expert competition. When I told him that, I think he swore in German," Jill said with laughter in her voice.

Damian already liked this woman, "You think? You don't speak German?"

"Nope. I like to think I can recognize swearing in any language though if you know what I mean."

Damian chuckled and said, "Yes. So Leticia thinks that your friend and I are brilliant IT geeks. Does she want us to compete in a geek-off or something?"

"No. I think she'd like you both to work for her. The FBI uses a few brilliant teenage hackers on occasion, but my friend Henrik Klein and you are on the next level."

Damian did a quick search on the physician and was

impressed with the weird cases she was involved in, and that was just a quick two-minute search. He now likewise took a moment to search for Henrik Klein. He recognized the name, but he didn't know where he'd heard it.

"I think I met your friend some time ago in another life. We do have similar computing abilities. However, I'm a lone wolf and he has a multi-national corporation behind him. I would enjoy meeting him again if he's ever in the San Francisco area."

"I'll let him know as he's all over the world, but I suspect he would like to meet you and probably hire you."

"Yes, well, forget that. I've turned down the FBI, the San Jose police, and many other people. I operate my small company churning out inventions and that's all I want to do. There is no salary that will change my thinking."

"Got it. Now on to John Baldwin. It sounds like a simple skier death has turned into a bigger case. Detective Severino described the fake-lawyer scenario and the evidence you found of him meeting the victim's former co-founder, Ryan. She also sent me the autopsy records as I'm boarded in Toxicology in addition to Forensic Pathology."

"And you operate a vineyard."

"So you did a search on me, as I did on you," she said.

"Of course, that's what computer geeks do. What are your thoughts about John Baldwin's death? I must say that I'm surprised it wasn't classified as a homicide at the time of his death as the circumstances demanded that."

"You can't declare a death a homicide without evidence of an intentional murder. All the findings from his case are circumstantial. So classifying his death as undetermined is the best the medical examiners could do in both counties. Here's the next problem: Most of the agents that I can think of that might cause his death are not provable this long after his death. Even if we exhumed the body today, many poisons wouldn't still be in his system. The two original MEs tested for standard poisons at the time."

"Let me back up. Do you think his death is a homicide?"

"Yes. Can I prove it? No. I'm a skier and there's no reason for his body to be in those skis at that scene without physical evidence. He didn't just drop out of the sky, dead."

"Okay. What are some of the agents that would have killed him without evidence, and then how would his body end up where it did? Did someone kill him elsewhere and carry his body there and dump it with ski boots and skis on?"

"That would be my guess. So, he could have been dosed with nitrogen gas, or a paralytic. He would have fallen asleep with nitrogen and never woke up. With a paralytic, his diaphragm would stop working and then his heart and brain would stop from a lack of oxygen. It would be a terrifying way to die."

"Yikes. I'll hope for the fall asleep method rather than your final moments spent panicking."

"Yes. I had a case early in my private consulting gig where a skier was shot with a poison dart containing a paralytic agent. In that case, we had evidence of an injection site. In this case, I'm not aware that either M.E. found any injection sites."

"I told Natalie that declaring this case a homicide wouldn't get us anywhere as it wouldn't identify the murderer. I wanted an opinion from an expert, which sounds like you, hoping that might give me additional clues to research, but short of doing a search for nitrogen gas purchases in California a decade ago, I don't have any new angles to search. Would you ask your IT expert to search anything for you that I haven't searched for yet?"

"The only thing I can think of is doing a facial recognition search for Ryan in the Lake Tahoe area at the time of John's death. I don't know what a criminal profiler would say about this case, but I think that John likely knew his killer. The company was poor at the time of John's death, so I doubt that

Ryan Alexander could have afforded someone to do his dirty work for him. I would also look for evidence of a disagreement between the two men. Thank you for looking into the widow's situation and fixing it. I find in many of my cases that someone adjacent to the murder victim is getting screwed and I like to see that they get justice."

"Thank you, Dr. Quint. This is helpful information, and I will look at the Ryan Alexander location angle."

They said their goodbyes and Damian had several notes he wanted to follow up on. He was amused that the FBI thought he and Henrik Klein were two of a kind.

# CHAPTER 8

*D*amian left his warehouse intending to head back to his island. It was Friday and it had been a busier week than normal, but he felt good. He'd helped Hermione's entire senior class, he'd helped a widow who wasn't getting her fair share of her husband's hard work, and he'd hired the right person to take his vendor booth to the next level for the CES in Vegas.

He really wanted to ask Marcus what the reaction to his lawsuit was, but he knew Marcus wouldn't violate attorney-client privilege and he saw that Grape AI had announced the lawsuit to the Securities and Exchange Committee and their stock price had dropped. He worried that would reduce the cut that Sara Baldwin would get, but the software was solid and if in the future the CEO was proved to be a murderer, the company would survive with new leadership. He sent his thoughts to Marcus that the CEO, and therefore the company's reputation, would suffer, and he should ask for a cash settlement and ongoing royalties from the company. That way even though the company would be devalued due to the CEO's actions, Sara would receive long-term payments.

By the time he reached home, he received an email from Marcus thanking him for his suggestion. Marcus also said that the case was bringing him joy. Damian interpreted that to mean that the reaction to his filing the lawsuit meant that Ryan Alexander now knew his fake attorney was no longer going to help him.

He checked in with Ariana and Hermione, where he was met with a request from their ward.

"My school computer science club wants to meet with you. They want to understand how you saved all our college careers. Are you available?"

He heard Ariana mumble in the background, "Oh boy!"

"Let me think about it. I don't want to turn your high school club into a bunch of geeks focused on hacking. There are ethics involved, and your age group is impulsive. Let me think if I can give them an overview of what I did without teaching them how to do it. Do you understand what I am saying?"

"Yes. There are some real geeks in that club and they could likely be bullied into changing grades if they knew how to do it. I wouldn't call it impulsive; rather, I would say that peer pressure is powerful."

"Exactly. Hacking is illegal for a reason and I won't be teaching anyone how to do that. If you want to be a hacker, go work for the FBI or CIA and let them monitor your online behavior. Let me see if I can come up with a lecture about the trouble you can get into by visiting the dark web."

"That makes sense. Thanks Damian."

"Are you a member of that club?" Damian couldn't remember her talking about it.

"No. That's not going to be my future focus and I have you for a resource for all things computer science. There's no need to take up my brain space with computer knowledge. It's limited, you know."

Damian chuckled and said, "No, it's unlimited disk space,

but I get you don't want a bunch of junk files in your cache making it harder to remember swim records."

"Exactly!"

Damian couldn't help but be reminded about how easy it was to raise this teenager. He thought about his elder child, whose life had been snuffed out before she'd made it to her teen years. He wondered if she would have belonged to the computer science club given that she shared his DNA. He would never know. He sighed and tuned back into the ladies.

"Damian?"

"Sorry, I was distracted. What did you say?"

"I need to leave for the East Coast on Tuesday for both business and personal, and I'll be gone till Sunday. Can you stay at my house and be Hermione's sole cheerleader at her game next week?"

"Of course. Do you need a ride to the airport?"

"No. I lined up a car service, but thanks for offering."

"Send me your schedule and Hermione's so I can add them to my calendar. Should I bring my boat or car over on Tuesday?"

"Probably your boat. It's the fastest way to work, right?"

"Yes."

"On this side of the bay, you can use my car or Hermione can drive you. I'm talking to a biotech company in Boston that may be interested in one of my start-ups and then visiting family in New York City."

Ariana had moved from New York City to San Francisco after her husband died. They had both been investors and advisors to start-up companies and had accumulated a nice slush fund from their wise investments. She still visited family on occasion.

Moving into her house was the best thing to do for Hermione given her school schedule, and it was what he had done in the past. Each day on the way to work he would stop at his island and feed Bella and Bailey. They would miss him a little, but as long as he provided them with fresh fish and dry kibble on daily stops, they were content. They killed lizards, frogs, and the occasional fish, but the fish almost had to jump on land before they could catch them. He could take them with him to Ariana's house, but they would be unhappy to be stuck indoors, and he feared that he would never see the pair again if he let them outside at her house.

They made plans for Saturday and ended their conversation. He had time on his hands and thought about what he should do with it. He didn't have any new projects going on at work and he wondered if there was anything in any of the crises he'd worked on this week that could turn into an invention to prevent similar things from happening to other people. He thought about the high school grade scandal, and that was easily solved by taking their transcripts offline. In the case of Sara Baldwin and other tech entrepreneurs, he thought he should probably write a book on the determination of partner shares. However, that was a waste of time as the issue was relevant to a small number of the population and Ryan Alexander was one of the most corrupt tech CEOs he had come across, and Sara wouldn't likely have discovered his words of wisdom.

That left the cold case of John Baldwin's death. So a guy ends up dead in a state park. Again, nothing to invent there that would have prevented his or any other person's death. From a science perspective, did the police need tools in the field to better diagnose potential causes of death? That was worth examining as he continued to help Natalie with cold cases. If the police had better at-the-scene tools, would they have figured out John's cause of death and labeled it a homicide immediately and performed more extensive poison testing? Would they have put more resources into the case earlier? He didn't think so, as two California counties had put medical examiner and detective resources at the time of the death. However, it wasn't as if knowing what caused John's death would help anyone find the murderer. So he put a kibosh on all his ideas related to this week's cases for new inventions. A brilliant idea that no one used didn't serve anyone.

So maybe he should give up on the ideas and focus his attention on Hermione's school hacker. As far as he knew, he was the only one who cared about why her school was hacked. He read that most school hackers were inside jobs. It would be amazing if he found a fellow student behind the hack, but in his reading, most inside jobs didn't target an entire graduating class. So he went to work searching for the hacker.

Just like his first search, he closed in on answers close to midnight. The hacker was from Russia, and the job seemed like it was ordered by the Malaysian pharmaceutical company that Hermione's parents tangled with a year or so ago. He sighed. He thought his earlier threats had shut down the company's attempts against Hermione. Then he had a thought—where was the court case her parents were involved with? Maybe that was the reason for the sudden interest in harming Hermione.

He did a search for the court case and had trouble finding it. Was it a state, local, federal, or international court? His eyes were burning from staring at his screen for too long. He decided to talk with Hermione about it. He knew that she spoke with her parents weekly and maybe they mentioned it. He closed everything down and went to bed. He could start again the next day.

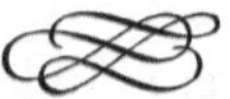

# CHAPTER 9

The next morning Damian was sitting on one of his island's rocks fishing for the cats. They were nearby watching intently whenever he brought a fish out of the water. Once the fish were swimming around in the water of his 5-gallon bucket, they ignored him and watched the movement in the bucket. He always found this amusing and wondered what was going on in their cat brains. They would reach forward and touch the rim of the bucket, squirm, pace, and return. It was a routine they had had since they arrived as a pair of adopted kittens to his island.

He finished up, making a note to himself to do a bunch of fishing the next day so he would have a supply of fish to leave for the cats when he stopped there each day on the way to work while staying at Ariana's house. He sliced up the fish outside at a tiny station he'd built for this exact purpose. There was no reason to stink up the inside of his house with fish guts. Once he was done filleting and providing fresh chunks of fish to the cats, he took the remainder inside and sealed a day's worth of fish in vacuum bags that he could break open each day for them. He supposed he could have fished off Ariana's dock before he boated across the bay each day, but there were different fish in her area and he didn't want to change the cats' diet.

He packed his overnight bag for the weekend and pointed his boat towards Ariana's dock. He would need to have the conversation with her at some point about the hacking scandal. If the school ever asked him if he had tracked down the hacker, he would say no. He knew that Hermione would be mercilessly bullied if word got out that she was the cause of the hack. He was 99% sure that the high school lacked the ability to trace the hack. Since he had fixed the transcript situation for the graduating class, there was no need for the school to look further.

When he arrived at Ariana's dock, he played fetch with Miguel on her beach. He went inside to greet the ladies and was pleased to find Hermione at home.

"Hermione, I have bad news. I spent several hours last night trying to track down the hacker of your high school transcripts. The hacker was located in Russia, but was hired by somebody in Malaysia. This makes me think it's your parents' old arch enemy —the Malaysian drug company."

"Really? They don't seem to want to give up. Should I mention that to my parents?"

"Maybe. I don't think the marshals will do anything different. Have you heard them mention that they have ever been in danger?"

"No. They do a great job protecting them. They've never mentioned having a problem."

"Is their court case getting close?"

"I never talk with them about it. I think they are so desperate to hear about my life outside of witness protection that they don't mention what's going on. I'm not supposed to talk with them for a week. Do you need me to make an emergency contact? I mean, my grades are safe, so I don't know that I care who hacked the transcripts."

"It's nice that we have your grades squared away, but what if they had hacked into your grades only? When those revised grades were sent out to colleges; you would never know until you started seeing rejections."

"That's true. I guess you need to put them out of business for me," Hermione said with a confident smile.

"You're sure I can do that?"

"Yes. You become a superhero when tasked with anything computer wise, so I'm sure that you can put the Malaysians out of business. Is there some way I can help?"

"No, but thanks for the vote of confidence. I think you would be wise not to let anyone at school know that I've found the hacker. It will go better for you if the others don't know that you were the catalyst for all this.

"The one thing you *could* do for me is ask your parents the next time you talk to them which court their case is in and are they getting close to testifying? These idiots from Malaysia have been quiet for over a year. I'm wondering what had them going after you at this time."

"That's a good question. I hadn't thought about that. I'm heading out to the movies with my friends and then we're spending the night at Charlie's house. I'll see you guys later."

The two adults watched the teenager walk outside to the garage and they soon heard the garage door opening. Damian looked at Ariana, who shrugged.

"I guess we should be happy that she has no lasting trauma from being nearly killed by the Malaysians," Ariana said.

"Yeah, I guess you're right. Why are they spending the night at a boy's house? What do you want to do this evening?"

"You're letting your age show. Charlie is a popular girl's name now. Let's head into the city for dinner at my favorite Italian restaurant and then maybe stroll along the Embarcadero afterward."

"Okay," Damian said, a little befuddled over the wide-ranging topics in the past ten minutes.

Ariana just smiled and went to grab her purse to drive.

The two of them had a nice evening, but Damian was like one of his giant computers with data running in the background. While enjoying his food and his time with Ariana, he was puzzling about what to do with the Malaysian criminals so he could fulfill Hermione's statement that he was a superhero when it came to data. He knew he needed to know what was going on with Hermione's parents' court case. He and Ariana did not have a path to converse with her parents. They knew she talked with them regularly, but they really had no need to talk with them themselves. He decided to reach out to the FBI agents who had investigated them to see if they could pass a message on to the marshals guarding her parents. He'd explain about the grade situation and where he traced it and asked them if it was related to the court case. He was sure he would hear back in a few days. That decision made, he returned his full attention to Ariana.

He enjoyed the remainder of the weekend with Ariana and Hermione once she returned home from her sleepover. There was no answer from his FBI contacts and he worried about how he was going to be Hermione's superhero. He returned home Sunday and would return to Ariana's early Tuesday. Crossing the bay was often thinking time for him as he'd made the trip now at least one hundred times. He had no inspiration about what to do with the Malaysian company for now.

After seeing Ariana off to the airport and Hermione to school, he headed to work. He was halfway there when his phone alarmed with an intruder alert. His island had been quiet the last year with no hostile or accidental visitors stepping on land. Who would be out near the island at this time of day? It was a workday, so there were few pleasure crafts on the bay. He slowed his boat and pulled up his camera. Someone was on his island's beach. They were covered head to toe in black and wore a mask, so an unfriendly person.

Damian opened his watercraft garage and launched a drone. The drone carried water balloons that he could drop on an intruder, staining them with an ugly green dye and lightweight GPS fibers so they could be tracked. Damian idled out in the bay as it was hard steering the drone and his boat with waves moving his boat back and forth. His drones were quiet and with the ambient noise of waves and winds, the intruder didn't hear the drone until a water balloon exploded on top of his head.

The intruder looked up and pulled a gun out of his waistband intending to shoot the drone down. Damian had armed his island well for protection. He had a series of water cannons that blasted people with unlimited water from the bay. It was a cold and high-pressure shower. He turned two cannons on the intruder and blasted away. Once he was done and before the intruder wiped the water from his eyes, he hit him with a second water balloon.

Anyone who caught a glimpse of Damian at this time would have seen a very satisfied smile on his face. He watched the intruder get back into his boat and leave, heading toward Oakland Damian guessed. He pumped his fist in the air that he had scared off another bad person thanks to his technology. He couldn't identify the intruder, but with the GPS fibers he should be able to trace where he went.

Damian continued his journey to his Richmond marina while monitoring the intruder's movement. He debated driving to work or following the intruder as he made his way through Oakland. After weighing the pros and cons, he decided to track the intruder by computer and see where he ended up. He would be stuck with the green dye for at least two days. The location where he stopped was the Cypress Housing Project, so likely the guy was a hired hand. Damian debated what to do with the recording of the thug. His island was governed by three counties. Should he talk to any of them? In the end, he decided to stay quiet. He doubted the thug would be back, and now he had a tracker on him for a few days. Damian decided to hire a private investigator to see who the thug met with until his GPS signal ran out and to also identify his visitor. He knew the guy didn't wake up that morning and decide to boat out to Damian's island and try to access it. He'd bet the intruder couldn't afford to rent the boat to get there.

In the past he would have dropped everything and followed this guy himself, but he had broader responsibilities now and this was something he would be better served to hire out. Fortunately, he knew someone who wouldn't be put off by Damian's tracking method and he agreed to the job.

With that taken care of, he returned to focus on his business. He had a staff meeting today and he wanted to discuss some new projects with his staff. He was interested in knowing if they had any ideas. All the projects they were presently working on were ideas he had started in his island lab. He would bet they had ideas on their own to pursue.

Hours later, he was impressed once again with the crew he'd hired. They did indeed have a fresh round of ideas to pursue. As each person suggested an idea, the others pitched in with ideas on how to make it better. They knew how to collaborate with each other, and no one's ego was in the way. He felt energized by his team, their ideas, and the future of his company.

Somehow, without noticing it, he changed from inventing things to pass the time while grieving for his family to feeling engaged and optimistic about the future. He had this group of brainiacs to thank in addition to Natalie, Ariana, and Hermione for getting him beyond the grief that had consumed him in the immediate years after his family's murder. In a rare moment of talking about his personal life, he thanked them for helping him heal.

Then he saw Chris, Angus, and Haley's faces and added, "No tears, folks. This is happy news. It's probably the only time I'll say something about it. Back to work."

He made a quick escape to his office to check on whether his private detective had any information on the intruder. He was pleased to see he had a name, address, and short bio on the guy. He was a thug with quite a criminal record. He wondered if the Malaysian drug company was behind this thug. The detective reported him as having bright green dye on his head and face. That comment brought a fierce grin to Damian's face. He liked that the hoodlum would have to explain the color on his face to everyone over the next few days. It would be hard to make up a story about the dye. His detective would follow the thug until the GPS crystals fell off his body. Prior experiments showed that would take three to five days. He hoped that this goon would meet with the client who hired him within that time span.

The remainder of the day was quiet, and he was soon boating across the bay to Ariana's house. She had made it safely to her meeting in Boston. He and Hermione would be reheating leftovers this night. Tomorrow, she had a water polo match, and they would dine out after the game. He arrived at the dock about ten minutes before his ward returned from practice. He was outside playing with Miguel who had been inside all day. His phone alarmed when Hermione's car passed the sensors in the driveway, so he wrapped up his play with Miguel and they went inside.

"Hey Kiddo, how was school and practice?"

"Since you saved my entire high school class's college futures, I am the queen of the class. I have the coolest dad on earth."

"Dang. Is there any praise higher from your generation?"

"I know, right. Seriously, my classmates are always asking how you did it and then they're disappointed that I can't describe it in detail. Can you give me a description for non-geeks so I can explain?"

"Sure. Just tell them I went into a deep dark hole of the web searching for data that contained your name, your science teacher's name, and one other student. Once my search turned up your names in a dark and dusty corner, I made a grab for the data. How does that sound?"

"That's actually an explanation I can remember and repeat. Thanks, Damian."

"Do you want to eat now or do some of your homework first?"

"I'm starving from practice, so let's eat now."

They cooked, chatted, played a round of video games, and then went to their rooms to do homework and work, and repeated the routine the next day.

# CHAPTER 10

On Thursday, Damian had some answers. His private detective submitted pictures of who the thug met with. Most of the pictures were of his neighbors in the Cypress Housing neighborhood. One picture featured him at Jack London Square talking to a white man. The green dye still marked his skin depending on how the sun hit it. Damian bet that by the end of the day, the GPS crystals would stop working. He hoped this picture would clue him in. He did a facial recognition search once he zoomed in on the picture. An answer came back and alarmed him.

It was Ryan Alexander, current CEO of Grape AI. He picked up his phone and called Marcus. He didn't have Sara Baldwin's telephone number, and he knew he could find it, but he also knew that Marcus would be of more help. He also sent a quick text message to Natalie.

Fortunately, Marcus answered his phone.

"Damian, what's up?"

"Marcus, you need to arrange protection for Sara. A couple of days ago I had an intruder approach my island. You may not know this, but I have significant protection systems on the island as the police response is slow to the island as I live out in the Bay. Anyway, I doused the intruder with a concoction of green dye and GPS crystals dropped from a drone. I hired a private detective to follow the guy and snap pictures. He lives in the Cypress Housing projects in Oakland, so I doubted he had the money to rent the boat to get to my island. One of the pictures the private detective took was of him meeting with Ryan Alexander in Jack London Square and . . ."

Marcus interrupted, "Sara Baldwin needs protection."

"Yes. I have a call in to the detective that I'm working with on the case of her husband's death. I suppose my name was listed as the computer expert when you filed the lawsuit?"

"Yes. I'm sorry that's caused you trouble."

"I'm well protected and Ryan Alexander has shown his hand. I'm most worried about Sara and her children. I can afford to hire private security for her family while the wheels of justice turn. Can you contact her and brief her on the situation? With teenagers in high school, it would be hard to relocate the family, but we could get some bodyguards for her by the end of the day probably."

"This is way beyond my level of expertise. Let me speak with her and a good friend who is a criminal attorney about our options. I'll get back to you and let you know what's going on."

They ended the call and Damian dialed Natalie's number.

"These cold cases always seem to affect you personally, Damian. I'm sorry."

"I'm not. I'm excited that we're bringing justice to Sara Baldwin and her family and exposing Ryan Alexander for the criminal that he is. I don't know if he killed John Baldwin or hired it out, but I'm going to find the connection. What I'm worried about is Sara and her kids. I contacted her attorney and informed him about what's going on. I told him I could afford to hire private security for Sara and her family. Can the Police Department increase their drive-bys to her house? Her attorney is going to contact a criminal attorney to see what our legal options are at this point. Do you have any suggestions?"

"I didn't expect all of this activity when I reopened this death case. Let me talk to my lieutenant about our options. You did a good job protecting my house when the crooks were after me and my family. Can you do the same for Sara in addition to the private security? I know teenage boys and they would likely be intrigued with your technology and you would make the family safer."

"Yes, I could do something for them. I don't feel comfortable calling Sara directly at this moment in time, so I'll contact her attorney and make the offer through him. Let me know what your lieutenant thinks."

Damian took a moment to consider what he had seen of Sara's house and the supplies he had on hand in his lab. He definitely could put intruder alarms around her house. He could even supply them with drones that dropped things on intruders. Those had to be handled manually, though, as the mail delivery person wouldn't appreciate being doused with skin staining dye. After gathering his plan based on his supplies and his knowledge of her house, he texted Marcus with his ideas. As Marcus was his patent attorney, he was used to the weird stuff that Damian could do. All he could do now was wait.

A few hours later he had his answers and he loaded stuff onto his truck to make the drive to San Jose. When he arrived, Sara's sons were with her and all three looked very concerned. After introductions were made, he sat down with the family.

"Marcus called me about what happened to you and what my options were. The first thing I did was bring the boys home from school. Marcus said that private security would be provided by this evening and that in the interim you had technology that would make my house safer."

"When we met earlier, you learned that I was a computer expert and that I have patents that Marcus represents me on, but I also have a lot of homegrown security systems that protect me. I live on a private island in San Francisco Bay and if anything happens there, the police response time is long and it's not their fault. It's my remote location."

"A few days ago, a man hired from the Oakland projects approached my island by boat. I have perimeter alarms and was notified. As the man was wearing all black including a ski mask, I knew he was up to no good. I launched a drone that carries water balloons filled with skin-staining bright green dye and containing GPS crystals."

The boys, whom he estimated to be near Hermione's age, both said, "That's so dope!"

Damian smiled and continued, "I then turned that over to a private detective who took pictures of anyone the man met with over the next couple of days. One of the pictures showed Ryan Alexander meeting with the man in Jack London Square. That's when I knew you needed additional protection. I contacted Marcus to explain the situation to him. I also contacted Detective Severino so that the San Jose police are on board and will increase surveillance on your house. I guess if there's any good news in this situation it's that although it took me two days to identify the intruder, no one bothered you in that time."

Sara had tears in her eyes and said, "I don't know what piece of karma created the opportunity for you to come into our lives, but I'm grateful you're here and looking out for our welfare. Should we go into hiding? I hate the thought of that as it would be so disruptive to the boys' lives."

"I thought of that and arrived at the same conclusion. My ward is in her senior year and to pull her out of school would screw up her college aspirations. How about if I add some technology to this house and show the boys how to use it? Then I have to run as my ward has a water polo match."

He got another affirmative response from the boys as their mom nodded agreement. He quickly set up the perimeter alarms, then he pulled a plastic container containing his special mixture of dye and GPS crystals. The balloons were made of a latex that was slightly thicker than the average water balloons. He showed them how to load it on the drone and then admonished them to not use it on each other. They were teenage boys, after all.

"You'll be grounded for a month if you use those balloons on anyone other than an intruder. Do you understand me?" Sara demanded looking into each boy's eyes. "This is a very serious situation, and you will treat it as such."

The boys nodded and looked at their mom with guilt on their faces. That told Damian that the moment he was gone, they had planned to use the drone and practice dropping it on each other. Fortunately, he foresaw the problem and brought some regular water balloons for them to practice with. He handed them over and the boys went outside to the backyard to practice.

"Will they be safe with your equipment and from any intruders?" Sara worried.

"They will. We can watch them while I show you how to set up the alarms on your phone. I want to show you how to make the system recognize the normal things in your yard like birds, dogs that routinely walk by, and so forth, so you don't get alarms for those things."

Damian proceeded to do that, taking an image of the first teenage boy in the backyard and labeling it as normal, then had Sara practice with the second boy. She seemed confident with the system and he moved on to the drone. He brought a controller with him for the drone rather than operating it from his cell phone. He knew the boys in the household might not have a phone and he wanted anyone to be able to operate it when need be.

The boys were returning inside and seeing how wet both of them were, he guessed that they had dumped two or three balloons on each other. He then showed the family how to load the special balloons and leave them on the back patio so that they would be ready to go if they were needed.

"Sara, do you feel like you know enough about these systems to show the bodyguards when they get here?"

"Yes I do. I use a lot of technology at work, so even though I'm old in the eyes of my boys, I'm pretty good on the uptake of new technology."

"If you don't have any further questions, then I have a water polo game to get to."

Sara looked at both boys and they all nodded that they felt comfortable with the systems he installed and the drone. She gave him a hug and had the boys shake his hand. She looked a lot more relaxed than when he arrived.

He was about to leave when she asked a question.

"Will I be able to go to work and can the kids go to school once the bodyguards arrive?"

"I'm not an expert at bodyguards, but the company has been contracted to supply whatever you need to continue your daily lives. So you'll get an escort to work and back, as will the kids to school and back. More than that, I don't know. I've never had a bodyguard," Damian smiled faintly, nodded to the family, and left.

Damian texted Hermione that he might be a little bit late to her game. He had a role in each game, which was to record it for the coach and for her parents. He drove as fast as he could, but traffic was notoriously congested in the Bay Area. Fortunately, the game was at her high school, which meant he didn't have to waste time looking for parking. He walked in as players were being introduced and proceeded to set up his tripod and camera to record the game. When he first started recording Hermione's games, he used his cell phone which had a great camera. Now he used a separate camera for the function so he could sit in the stands and remotely control it.

He waved to the other parents and relaxed that he had made it on time. He was one of those people who hated to be late to anything. He'd asked Sara to text him when her bodyguards arrived as he wanted to make sure that the ball wasn't dropped on that concern. Just before halftime, he got the text and relaxed further.

There was a short halftime which gave the kids a chance to use the bathroom and grab a drink and then they were back out in the pool. The score was tied at the half, but Hermione's coach gave the better halftime speech and soon they were dominating the other school. After the game was over, he began disassembling the camera and tripod. He looked for a nod from Hermione that she still wanted to meet him for pizza at her favorite restaurant. Last season she didn't have a driver's license. Now that she did, she would meet him there and get her pizza faster as he didn't have to wait for her to shower before setting out to the restaurant.

He sat down in a booth to read his emails and waited for her arrival. He had an empty cup waiting for her to fill it with her favorite beverage. He was deep into reading and jumped when she put a hand on his shoulder. He hadn't even noticed when she entered the restaurant.

They both said "Sorry" at the same time and then smiled.

"What did coach say at halftime?" Damian asked.

"He pointed out what we all should have noticed. They had one good hitter on their team and everyone sent balls her way. So we defended her instead of everyone else and that greatly decreased the goals on the other team."

"I should have paid attention to that. For the most part, you all look the same in the water. I should have been looking at your numbers on your hats as I would have picked up on that."

"I think we all saw that they had one really good striker on their team, but it's too early in the season for us to pick up on the logic of just blocking balls getting to her instead of trying to block the whole team. You ordered the pizza already, right?"

"Of course. I think it might be coming our way right now," Damian said, looking over her shoulder. He shoved the cup at her and said, "You might want to fill your cup up. I know you have a special mix you like."

"You didn't order wine for me?"

"Gee whiz, Ariana and I give you wine one time and you think you can drink it regularly."

"Just saying that if I was a kid in Italy, I could be pairing my pizza with wine."

"I think if you were a kid in Italy, your hair wouldn't be wet at the moment as you wouldn't have played high school water polo."

"True that," she said as she took an appreciative sniff of the pizza just put in front of them. She dashed off to fill her cup while he placed a slice on her plate and then his.

"How did your day go? Are you any closer to figuring out what killed that skier?"

He had told her about the skier a week ago and then remembered he hadn't told her about the intruder on his island.

"I still don't have any answers about his death. I don't think I told you about what else is going on with that case. The guy was the original engineer for an AI company that had an independent stock offering. He left behind a wife and two children, and they got nothing more than a life insurance policy."

"That's not right!"

"Yes, and there's more. The AI company set her up with a fake attorney who filed a fake lawsuit to get a share of the money, and time was running out on the lawsuit. I figured out what was going on and set her up with my intellectual property attorney and I gave him the analysis that should help her get a rightful share of the stock offering, or about fifty million dollars. Now I think the current CEO might have killed the engineer or hired someone to do it. I had an intruder a couple days ago approach my island dressed all in black."

Hermione showed a brief tensing that he might have been in trouble and then she relaxed knowing the tools he had at his fingertips to defend his home.

"So the intruder walked away with green dye and GPS crystals on his face or body somewhere," she said, completing the story.

"Yes, he was a thug with a criminal record. I hired a private detective to follow him around and received a picture of him meeting with said CEO in Jack London Square."

"I can't believe you forgot to tell me this story. What happened next?" Hermione asked, working on her second piece of pizza.

"I just came back from San Jose. I set up perimeter alarms and gave them a drone that would drop my special water balloons on any intruders. I also had the attorney set up bodyguards for the family. It will take a while, but that CEO is going to get criminally charged and the engineer's widow should end up financially set for life with the fifty-million-dollar payout."

"Wow, you've been a superhero twice this month. You saved my high school class, then you saved a family. I'm really proud of you. Can you explain how you solved the problem to my computer science club?"

"I haven't solved it yet, but I think the moral of the story is you can choose to do good or bad with your computer skills. I hope all your classmates choose good."

*D*amian was driving north across the Richmond San Rafael bridge, having seen Hermione off to school. He got an email from Natalie that his car read to him about an incident at the Baldwin house the previous night. Apparently, all the precautions he put in place to protect the family were most timely. The bodyguards took down an intruder after one of the boys busted a water balloon over his head. The intruder was currently residing in the Santa Clara County Jail. He had a criminal record and refused to talk. Law enforcement hoped to learn more about him after a public defender visited him. The DA was preparing a few different options with offers on the table if he revealed who hired him.

Damian used the drive to think about the original case—the death of John Baldwin. He suspected they were going to be able to connect Ryan Alexander to these thugs, and that would see him arrested for attempted murder if the intruder had any weapon on him. However, he would like to see him put away for a long time, and he wanted resolution for the family about what happened to their husband and father.

He pondered where they were on the case. Natalie should be receiving any records that the telephone company still had for John's cell phone at the time of his death. Then he thought of something else to investigate. What if he hacked into Ryan Alexander's bank account to see what he spent money on around the time of John's death? That's, of course, assuming he didn't change banks in the past decade, but then most people didn't change banks according to his research. Maybe there was evidence that he was in the Lake Tahoe area, which would be a starting place. He brought his truck to a halt at the next exit, and he set his computer to work. Hopefully by the time he reached his office, his computer would have found the answer. Then he had a second idea which he wrote down before powering up his vehicle to continue the journey.

Damian arrived at the office and looked at his search. If there was evidence that Ryan Alexander was in the Lake Tahoe area, then Natalie might be able to subpoena the official records rather than his own illegally gotten records. After a few more tweaks, he had what he was looking for—gas and toll road records indicating that he did indeed drive toward Lake Tahoe the day of John's death.

After the IPO, Ryan had the cash to hire others to do his work. However, at the time of John's death, they were a very poor company. The cycle of start-ups was to start with an idea that fixed a problem for the customer, usually in technology, while you were a starving student and worked eighteen hours a day pursuing that idea. Once an inventor had what was called a minimum viable product, then they used data to calculate a demand for the product. After that, they moved on to seeking seed funding in the amount of two to four million dollars on average. John was doing presentations for that seed stage. His wife's job paid the bills. Within three months of John's death, one of the companies he had presented to awarded them seed funding of four million dollars.

Ryan was also married at the time and his wife supported the family. Somewhere between the seed stage and the IPO, he divorced his wife. The settlement was public, and he learned that she got little as the seed funding was tied to the company, not Ryan.

Damian arrived at his office and his computer was still working through name and password combinations. So he did a separate search on Ryan just to see what the general news was about him. A short time later, he had a dismal picture of the man.

After reading all the reprehensible things that Ryan Alexander did, he wished he could go back and fix things for more people whom he had screwed. Damian was surprised that Ryan hadn't screwed the company up in the years since. However, he noted that the wise seed investor demanded approval of a new engineer to protect their investment. That engineer was still there and was well paid. He had to think that after all the time with Ryan Alexander as his boss, the engineer might be as corrupt as the CEO.

His computer clicked that the search was complete. It found the username and password combo that allowed Damian to get into Ryan's old bank records, and there was the information he was looking for. Besides being a crook, he was a stupid crook at that. He had lots of activity on his card around the time that John died in and around South Lake Tahoe. It was proof of nothing more than a possibility that he could be a suspect. Damian needed more information about the scene of his death.

He pulled up the pictures that Natalie sent him. There were footprints from the parking lot and then many footprints around John that were likely first responders and the police. Did he have the story wrong? Did the guy put his shoes on, then walk over to the trail and his footprints were lost among the first responders?

Maybe it was a Dr. Jill Quint question—could you get shoes

on a dead person? If you couldn't, then John put his shoes and skis on himself and then keeled over. If that was the case, then did the killer meet John on the trail and kill him with something untraceable? He picked up the phone and punched the forensic pathologist's number into his cell and waited for her to pick up. He lucked out when she answered.

"Hey, Jill, it's Damian and I've got a question for you. Did John Baldwin die wearing his ski boots and skis?"

"Yes, that's what the crime scene pictures show."

"Let me be more specific. Can you get ski boots on a dead person?"

"That's an interesting question. It would depend on how close to the time of the death that someone tried to put boots on the person. I would say that if they did it within an hour of death probably. Any time after that, depending on the victim's age, general health, and ambient temperature, rigor mortis or tissue swelling would prevent getting a boot on a foot. It would be easier with a shoe. I'd also say the medical examiner might not notice the position of the foot in a shoe depending on what the first responders had to do at the scene. When I think back to my cases over the years, I can't remember paying attention to see if the heel was in the shoe and the laces or buckles were tight enough to hold the foot in position. Sorry, I can't give you a more definitive answer. In the case of mortuaries, sometimes they burial people without shoes, sometimes the deceased wear shoes, and sometimes, shoes are in the casket next to the feet; it depends on the condition of the body and what the family wants."

"After listening to the variables you've listed, I'm not sure it makes a difference. One more question about DNA: If you have a co-worker, does their DNA necessarily slough off on you? I'm asking a really far-fetched question of if we exhumed John Baldwin's remains and found Ryan Alexander's DNA on him, I assume that simply being co-workers would be the cause of that unless John had taken several showers and hadn't been near Ryan for, say, seventy-two hours."

"Part of my forensic pathology training and experience is understanding what would hold up in court. If I exhumed the body and found Ryan Alexander's DNA on John, and made the statement that this was suspicious, my testimony would be blown up and my reputation would suffer as an expert witness."

"I figured you would say something like that. Let's just say I've got data that Ryan Alexander was in the area at the time of John's death. I'm trying to figure out how to link that to anything. I guess I'm saying that he had the opportunity; now I'm trying to find the means and motive."

"Maybe see if you can find any information about the relationship of the two men. This might help you find a better motive than Ryan was a scumbag."

Damian chuckled, "Sadly, that's where I'm at. I think you have the easier job with current cases. Finding data on these cold cases is a pain."

They chatted a little more, then ended the call.

Natalie dropped him another email with the news that the telephone company routinely deleted their records after three years. Still, their IT person had tried to find old data, but even after an extensive search, they could not find any records. Damian wasn't surprised by that result. He thought it would be a long shot to find old cell phone records.

Besides being a scumbag to his ex-partner's wife, he bet that Ryan lacked ethics with other people. At least if he got a few opinions, Damian would know if his impression of Ryan was right. Then he thought about going after the company's servers to see what was in their email system for around the time of John's death. There wasn't a system so far that he couldn't hack, and digital stuff never went away so even if Ryan deleted messages from around that time, he would still find them.

The most difficult part of this search would be the domain.

At the time of John Baldwin's death, the company was called Sunnyside AI, but now it was Grape AI. Sunnyside AI was such a stupid name that Damian thought that no one else would buy that domain name, so at least that was in his favor. He dug into the dark corners of the web to see if he could find the old data.

Damian looked up when someone knocked on his door. It was Lily.

"You look like you're chasing ghosts on your computer screen," she said.

"I'm looking for an old domain to find its email content. So I suppose that is chasing ghosts. What's up?"

"Two things. One, Jacob would like you to come talk to his computer science class. . ." She broke off when she saw Damian's smile. "What?"

"I got the same request from Hermione. I wonder if the two of them are sharing information."

"Probably. They are friends after working together last summer. You should consider it an honor that they asked. Jacob asked me to talk to his school's advanced math class. It's not a class in which he is in attendance, so I can't embarrass him as a parent. I guess you're cooler than I am," she said with a smile.

"Life with teenagers. What's the second thing?"

"I need some help with my project. I want to do a ton of boring repetitive testing with what I've created. This is a decent job for a science student."

"A student by the name of Jacob?"

"Probably not. I'd rather not share a parent and boss title over my son. I was thinking of reaching out to the university. What would be your requirements, and can we afford that?"

"They would have to sign a confidentiality agreement, so they need to be over 18 to sign documents. Yes, we can afford to hire them. Do a little research and set the wage that you need to find the right person. Since this is a short-term project, I would be more likely to pay a little more than the going rate for this job. I'll drop a line to Ariana so she can handle the personnel component whenever you find the right person."

"Thanks! I'll ask Jacob for a date and time to do a talk with his class and let you know."

"How long do you think the testing will take?"

"I assume a student can work a few hours after school and perhaps the weekend. So maybe two months once I find the person."

"Do you think it will be ready for prime time at the CES show? We could add your project."

"I hadn't thought that far ahead. Let me look at my project schedule again. I might be able to reasonably demo it at the show, but I want to confirm that I'll be ready. When do I have to give you a definitive answer?"

"Perhaps a week before the show. We can always add you to the booth at the last minute, but I think your friend Emily needs some time to get the right stuff in place to make it shine."

"I should be able to let you know a full month in advance, and maybe even two months if my testing goes well."

"That's good news. Have Jacob's teacher reach out to me to arrange a lecture. It will be different from the one I'm giving Hermione's school. As her entire senior class got hacked and had their transcripts removed, my presentation is almost more a mental health intervention for the sanity of the parents and students. So with them I'll be vaguely talking about how I found their grades in the deep corners of the web. I can address any topic and I'd like to know what the teacher wants me to touch on."

"Will do, and thanks for getting me some help."

Damian went back to trying to find the data associated with the old domain. There was something called the Wayback Machine which included old website archives, so he went there to see if he could find any data from the company. The archive started about a decade before the demise of Sunnyside AI, so the old website might have been saved.

The first place he looked showed nothing, but then he remembered Sunnyside AI was in a start-up in the W Combinator, an organization that housed start-ups. He'd bet that they contributed to the Wayback Machine. He kept up the search for a while longer and then realized he'd better get across the bay to get home before Hermione arrived at Ariana's house. He could continue his search once she retreated to her room to do homework.

He made a quick stop at his island to feed his cats and grab some clean clothes and was soon on his way to Belvedere. He docked his boat just as he saw the driveway camera indicate that Hermione was pulling into the garage. They met inside before Damian immediately took Miguel outside for play time. Someone was checking on the dog at midday, but he was sure the dog missed Ariana. Hermione followed him outside and they discussed their days.

"Did you tell Jacob about my lecturing your computer science club?" Damian asked.

"No, I haven't texted with him in a month or so. He's behind me a few years, so we don't have that much to chat about. Why?"

"I was invited to lecture at his school, and I figured he got the idea from you."

"No, I didn't mention anything to him. You should lecture my school first."

"Why?"

"This might seem weird, but as a form of counseling. Some of my classmates are still traumatized from learning that their transcripts had disappeared. All along I knew you could fix the problem, so I didn't stress over it, but some of my classmates were talking about suicide if you didn't find our grades. I think the majority of them were joking, but some students are more fragile than I am."

"That's terrible. Is your school getting some help for those kids who might need some extra help?"

"Yes, it's available, but I think your lecture might help."

"Everyone should know that throughout their lives, there will be someone around you who can work magic with a computer. In fact, some of your classmates may become that expert."

"Whatever. I know it won't be me."

"What are you thinking of going to college for other than swimming?" Damian asked. She had changed her opinion a few times since she had been his ward.

"While I'm pretty good at the science thing, it's not my passion. I thought about doing something in game design, but again, computers are not my passion. Besides, I'll have you for any computer needs. I'm thinking about law school at the moment, and that's what I'm putting on my college applications."

"Where else besides UC Berkeley are you applying?" Damian felt bad for not having this conversation with her earlier as he might have provided some guidance.

"I don't feel comfortable straying too far from you. These people after my parents aren't letting up, and if I need your help, I don't want to be across the country. Besides, maybe by the time the court case is finished, I'll have my bachelor's degree and then I can go anywhere for law school. So I'm also applying to Stanford, UC San Francisco, Santa Clara University, University of San Francisco, UC Davis, and the University of the Pacific."

Damian had no idea that the Malaysian pharmaceutical company thugs had created such insecurity for her. Then again, even before her parents were kidnapped, she'd been living a life on the run with her parents.

"So are you looking at a degree in political science? What's your first choice?"

"Maybe. My first choice is UC Berkeley. I've thought about what kind of lawyer do I want to be. I know I don't want to do criminal law. Estate planning sounds boring. I was actually thinking about something like patent protection. I could become your lawyer and do the same thing for Ariana's start-ups. So I might get a degree in science to help me understand patents."

Damian was impressed with her thinking and was pleased that she intended to keep Damian and Ariana in her life for a long time.

"Would you like me to contact Marcus Blackstone, who is my current patent attorney, to see if he would mind you spending a day with him?"

"That would be cool. Just don't tell him I want to replace him."

"I won't tell him that. All of the patent and intellectual property attorneys in this area are part of lawyer groups. Maybe if you do well in law school, his firm will hire you. Just working for Ariana and me won't be enough work for you. Then again, maybe you want to coach high school sports on the side and only work part time."

"Yes, that would be a dream, but I wouldn't be able to afford the rent or eventually buy a house if I did that."

"Gee whiz, Kiddo, you're really practical. How does someone your age know about paying rent and housing prices?"

"It's one of our classes in high school. They teach rent, paying bills, interest, loans, insurance. It's very practical."

Damian was still shaking his head as he asked, "What do you want for dinner?"

"Could we just have our food delivered? I would love some sushi or Chinese food."

"Yes, we can do that. I'm so used to living on my island that I forget you can have food delivered. Do you have any menus here anywhere?"

Hermione went to a drawer and pulled out a few menus, then found the one she wanted for her favorite restaurant. They settled on a Japanese restaurant and soon ordered their meals. She retired to her room to do homework until the food arrived about half an hour later.

The previous night Damian had sliced and diced law school information and created a chart with Hermione on school rating and athletics. The kid was right to target UC Berkeley—it suited all of her needs. He gave her the chart the next morning, and like any good teenager she rolled her eyes but put it in her backpack and left for school.

Damian smiled and left the house in the opposite direction to stop on his island and then move on to the marina and his vehicle to drive to work. He was the last to arrive which was the nice thing about owning the company—he could come and go as he pleased. He checked in with everyone and Lily gave him the teacher's number to call and arrange a presentation to Jacob's school. He likewise heeded Hermione's words about her class needing his lecture to heal from the trauma of their transcripts being lost and called the teacher at her school first.

He was on the calendar for her school the next day and Jacob's the day after. Both teachers were looking at essentially the same lecture. He would tweak them based on the school and was told to expect about fifteen kids in each class. After giving thought about what to say that would expand the students' minds without teaching them how to go places they shouldn't, he was ready to go with his presentation. He would bring his laptop and would lecture on the evils of the dark web to discourage any of the students from being hackers, which was, after all, criminal activity.

He then turned back to searching for the lost emails of Sunnyside AI. While the Wayback Machine contained earlier versions of the website, he had to search longer for individual emails. After hours of searching, he was going to give up as, without an active domain, he couldn't find old emails. He did find email addresses, though, from the old website. One of the earliest versions of Sunnyside AI listed the staff and their email addresses. He'd bet that those addresses were migrated over to Grape AI. He also compared the list to who now worked at Grape AI, and none of the original players were still there except the engineer that Ryan had hired to replace John Baldwin.

Damian next researched who the IT specialist was at the time of the transition of company names. With start-up companies, it was not an engineer who would design a company website; it was usually a marketing person. The company website was different from an app that the start-up company might be creating. The website was there to explain their technology and any pricing plans. So likely the engineer who replaced John didn't handle the migration to a new domain. Damian decided he needed to know the name of the website person.

He started a search for every address to see who the person was behind the address. Were they an engineer, a marketing person, personnel, or something else? Fortunately, when he went back to the early websites found at the Wayback Machine, he soon had a list of employees and their jobs. First he verified that none of the people in the original Sunnyside AI were still working for Grape AI. That was curious but not entirely unexpected. Some start-up staff were serial entrepreneurs. Also, the personality it took to get a business off the ground wasn't necessarily the personality type to sustain the business. As there were only six people and one was dead and the other in his mind a suspect that left four people to run down.

Before he picked up the phone, he needed to think about his conversation with these people. He couldn't imagine anyone giving him honest answers about Ryan Alexander and John Baldwin if he just cold-called them. Maybe this was a duty better handled by Natalie Severino. She at least had the power of the badge behind her. With that in mind, he described each person's background and contact information and asked the retired detective to make the calls. He added a few questions that she wouldn't necessarily think of and then decided he'd done all he could on that project.

He left his office to check on his employees. It was like a brain refresh to knock the cobwebs out of his brain from seeking a way to find John Baldwin's murderer, to using his computer and engineering skills to improve his inventions. He was working on a solar energy system that was designed to solve a certain problem—that of short days or overcast skies. The short-day issue was for the northern cities of the world and overcast skies were for those cities subject to fog and clouds like San Francisco. How did a panel absorb more light energy? After talking over the project with Angus, who planned to test the system on a northern Scottish island that was above the 60$^{th}$ parallel, he thought they would have a solution, and that excited him. Angus planned to visit the northernmost Shetland Island where their winter days were less than six hours by the end of December. The company had rented a home there and Angus would do a live demo showing how much the new panel was absorbing and powering the house. Solar could really help the economy on the small island and many other places around the world.

Despite handing off the interview work to Natalie, Damian was still thinking about the crime scene and how he could find evidence. He returned to the credit card activity that he found for Ryan Alexander and took a look at the geographical locations of those expenditures. Maybe that would tell him something. Lining up the charges, he could see that Ryan left the Bay Area to drive to Lake Tahoe on the day of John's death. He paid a bridge toll and used some of the freeway express lanes, paying tolls therein. He stopped for gas in the Sierra foothills town of Placerville and likely continued from there to South Lake Tahoe. As it was winter, Damian searched for the historical weather report for the day of John's murder. Ryan traveled along Highway 50 and each winter it would be closed off and on due to snowfall as the highway traveled through an altitude of more than 7,000 feet. The weather report showed the pass as clear for several days before and after John's death. So Ryan could have murdered his co-founder and not have stayed overnight in the region.

Damian again pulled up pictures of the scene. He thought the words *crime scene*, but at the time of John's death it wasn't clear that his demise was a crime. So how did the crime play out? Ryan probably communicated to John that he was joining him in Lake Tahoe to discuss the upcoming IPO or something equally important. Perhaps he suggested that they discuss it while cross-country skiing at Emerald Bay State Park. He could have said he wanted to stretch his legs after the drive and not interfere with John's time on the ski slopes. If he had been in John's shoes, he wouldn't have seen anything weird in that request.

So, the two men parked their cars. Wait, John's car wasn't near the park—it was back at the condo. So Ryan had to have offered to pick him up at the condo. Maybe he offered John a drink that had poison or a sedative in it. Damian didn't like that idea. If John felt sleepy in the car, he would have canceled their cross-country skiing trek and asked Ryan to take him back to the condo. Maybe he took a flask of John's favorite whiskey and poisoned that. If he took a sip just after they put on their skis at the edge of the parking lot, it would make sense that he dropped where he did. If that was the way the situation happened, Ryan must have had something to cover up the ski tracks. As the picture did not show two sets of tracks, that is the only thing that made sense. Most skiers come off the ski hill thirsty, so John would likely sip any beverage given to him.

Of course, this was useless information as he couldn't prove that any of it had occurred. At least he had thought of a scenario in which John could die with little evidence left behind. Now the question was, how could he prove Ryan's involvement? What if he still had the flask—could the murder weapon be at his house? Would whatever poison was used to kill John still be detectable in a flask? That was likely a question again for Dr. Quint. He dropped her an email with what he speculated had happened, and then asked about flasks, alcohol, poisons, and time.

An email arrived from Marcus indicating that another effort to hurt Sara Baldwin had been blocked. Damian picked up the phone and called him. He was considering moving her and her kids into protective custody, but it would mess with their school schedules, and the security and bodyguards were doing a good job of keeping the family safe. A bomb threat was called in to the police for the building that his law practice was in which disrupted his day, but otherwise Marcus was amused by the case.

Damian thought about adding protection for Marcus, but the lawyer could take care of himself, so he wasn't going to worry. Instead, he changed the subject and asked about internship opportunities.

"My ward is a senior in high school and told me yesterday that she was thinking about law school and in particular focusing on intellectual property. Do you have any career days to give high schoolers a glimpse of what you do as a lawyer?"

"I forgot you had a ward. We have a 'bring your child to work day' in the spring for our employees. As my kids are grown and out of the house, I can bring your ward to work in lieu of my own adult children. I'll find out the date of that event and let you know. Is she hoping to replace me as your lawyer?"

Damian chuckled and said, "How did you know? She said she wanted to work independently and just handle legal issues that Ariana and I have. I told her that wasn't enough work and the way your law practice worked, you employed science experts to be able to argue over patents. She said that she was looking at an undergraduate degree in a science field, so she'd be good in that area."

"I'm impressed with her well-thought-out life plan. That's at least seven years from now and I might be retired by then, so I have no competition from her."

"I would love to see her work in a large firm for many reasons, so hopefully her experience with your firm will make her want to work for a large firm and have more clients than just Ariana and me."

"It's never easy guiding a teenager on a future career path. I know; I had to contend with my kids when they were contemplating their futures," Marcus said.

"Did any of them become lawyers?"

"Nope. I have a nurse, an engineer, and a pilot."

"Good job, Marcus!"

They talked about a patent that Damian had recently applied for and then ended the call.

Before he could forget to tell Hermione, he sent her a text about hooking her up with Marcus in the spring. It was better for her to know what she wanted to do with her life, rather than changing her college major a few times. Then again, it was hard to make up your mind at 17 about the rest of your life. She probably needed to learn what the adjunct staff did to help the lawyers in the firm win intellectual property cases.

He was about to immerse himself in work when his alarm went off reminding him that he needed to meet Hermione at Ariana's house. He grabbed his stuff and rushed out of the office. Ariana would be back on Sunday, and he wouldn't be leaving so early next week.

# CHAPTER 13

With a lot of hustle on his end, he made it home and had just enough spare time to feed his cats and grab clothes for the next day. As he was lecturing at Hermione's school, he wanted to look respectable; not that he didn't usually, but as he thought about wearing a tie, he decided that wasn't the dress code for computer nerds in Silicon Valley. He had his laptop and an outline of his lecture written down. He would demo some parts of the internet, but he wanted to spend the majority of his time warning Hermione's classmates away from the dark web and its dangers.

He cooked burgers on the barbecue while Hermione air-fried French fries. After eating and clearing up their meals, and spending a short time on video games, Hermione retired to her room to complete her homework. Damian went over his presentation one more time. He was about to chase down the Malaysian hacker again, but he had an incoming email from Natalie with new information. The interviews were universally the same. None of the ex-employees liked Ryan Alexander as he was irrational and a back-stabber. They loved working with

John and were devastated by his death as they then had to deal with Ryan.

All the employees left the company shortly after John's death. One of those employees was in charge of the company's website domain. Even though she was told not to migrate all the old emails to the new domain once they changed the company name, that employee saved all the old emails onto a disk that she offered to Natalie. Damian picked up his cell phone to call her.

"Natalie, you need to get your hands on that disk as soon as possible. I don't know what you have to do on your end for the chain of custody for a future court case, but either I can come get a copy of it under the eagle eye of the detectives or you can just send me a copy."

"Let me ask my fellow detectives what to do in this case, as you're right that the chain of custody is very important if we're to use it as evidence against Ryan in the future."

"So he wasn't much liked when the company was Sunnyside AI?"

"Not at all. He took credit for anything that went right and had a temper tantrum for everything that went wrong. These employees said that you should expect at least half of what you do to be the wrong thing in a start-up company. Furthermore, even though Ryan expected perfection from the staff, he wouldn't admit to mistakes he made and they would have to go around him to get something working again. Two of them said Ryan Alexander was a life lesson and they've made sure when they've gone on interviews for other companies that they don't have to work with somebody like him."

"The man has no friends. He has a bad code of ethics that makes people stay away from him. I haven't heard anyone say a kind word about his contribution. I've wanted to make him our murderer simply because he's such an awful human being, but I suppose that won't get us anywhere in court. I hacked into his credit card records and I can prove he was in the Lake Tahoe region on the day of John's death. Of course, since I've hacked, I know you'll eventually need to get a search warrant to get the information from a legitimate source."

"In detective speak, we look for means, motive, and opportunity. Right now, we know Ryan had the opportunity, and I would guess the motive is related to money. The question is: How did he do it?"

"I was thinking about that earlier today. Here's my thought: He notifies John that he's on his way to Lake Tahoe to discuss something regarding the company. He also says he wants to stretch his legs because he's had a three or four hour drive to Lake Tahoe. He tells John he's going to pick him up and asks him to bring his cross-country skis for a short workout at Emerald Bay State Park while they chat. John being the snow enthusiast agrees. Once they get to the park, they put on their skis and boots and start moving forward from the parking lot. Then Ryan offers John a drink. Perhaps it's alcoholic, perhaps not, but most skiers are thirsty after a day of skiing. The drink has poison in it and John starts to feel bad a short time later and collapses. Ryan leaves him there to die and his remains to freeze overnight. Meanwhile he heads back to the Bay Area as the roads are clear and traffic is light in that direction at that time of the night. He probably thought that no one would notice his absence for the nine or so hours it likely took him to kill John Baldwin."

"Okay, that's doable, but what was his murder weapon and where is it now?" Natalie asked.

"I don't know. I was going to send another email to Dr. Jill Quint and get another read on the situation. I'm hoping that in his arrogance, Ryan kept the flask."

"Not to throw cold water on you, but this could all be just fantasy. I agree with your scenario of how it could have happened, but we lack the evidence at the moment to prove any of it."

"True, but we'll see once you get that disk. I think there had to be some angry conversations on it. Are you sending out a police officer to pick it up from the ex-employee's residence tonight? You should. It could break the case wide open."

"I'll do that. Then I'll need an outside computer expert to examine the disk and files to authenticate them. I can't use you as an expert as you've never registered your skills with a law enforcement agency. I know that you would do that for me, but I think we have a few other experts we can use."

"Yes, I want to avoid giving testimony in court, and you're correct that there are many people in this area who could verify the veracity of the disk. When your detective picks up the disk, ask him to ask the ex-employee to use the cloud to send you a copy of what's on it."

"I don't know what that means, but I'll ask her to do that."

"Just call me and I'll walk you through how to do it. I should be able to tell you overnight if there's something damning on the disk. If there is, you may want to arrange protection for that ex-employee."

"Okay, let me get moving on your requests."

"Thanks, Natalie."

After Damian ended the call, he was optimistic that the old email files might reveal what the relationship was like for the two men. Then he thought of one other thing to look for. He reached out to Sara Baldwin in an email to see if she kept paper copies of the cell phone bills from the year that John died. It was a long shot, but people tended to keep tax files for long periods of time. He knew it might take her a while to search for that piece of information and she may never have saved it, but it was worth asking for.

Damian wrote an email to the toxicologist, Dr. Jill Quint. He described the scenario that he had explained to Natalie. His question for her was, if it went down that way, what poisons could be put in a flask and be fast acting and not necessarily add a noticeable taste to what was in the flask. He looked at the clock and it was approaching 8:00 at night, so he didn't expect a response from her that evening.

He was pleasantly surprised when an hour later two emails hit at the same time. The esteemed Dr. Jill Quint had replied to his questions as well as Natalie sending directions for him to access the files of the old domain for Sunnyside AI. He opened the doctor's email first as it was likely short and sweet. He was correct in that she provided a list of poisons that would work under the scenario he described. She also indicated which ones might have been detected in an autopsy and others which could be detected in an autopsy but were not routinely tested for. It was good information.

He moved on to Natalie's email. She had attached a copy of the domain's data from the ex-employee. She also mentioned that her department was having a conversation with the District Attorney on the legality of obtaining this information. Damian hadn't thought about that question, but he supposed that the police could be accused of getting it illegally. Oh well, that piece of this murder investigation wasn't under his control or anything that he was knowledgeable about.

He sorted the emails focusing on the month before John Baldwin's death. He could see the two co-founders were having arguments about the technology, the name of the company, and how the start-up employees would be compensated once the company went to IPO. John was interested in sharing the proceeds with all the employees. Ryan wanted just three people rewarded. They continued arguing about the arrangement and then John threatened to alert the equity company that had given them seed funding. Ryan had named the company Sunnyside AI and was disagreeing with John's desire to change the name to Grape AI which was more representative of the industry they served. Ryan didn't have a plausible reason for rejecting the name change, it seemed that it was entirely about his ego. It was curious that the name actually changed after John's death. Damian wondered if the name change came from the engineer or the seed investor. Finally, the two of them disagreed on how the technology worked. Ryan wasn't an engineer and he made no effort to understand what John was saying about the application they were engineering. Damian could see that these two were headed for a business divorce. Ryan must have seen it also and decided to make the divorce happen on his terms.

He dropped an email to Natalie with his impression of what was in the files and the fact that he would look at them more the next day. He needed to go to sleep so he would be on his game for the lecture at the high school. His appointment was at nine, but Hermione had an 8 am class, so he had a quiet house to practice his lecture before leaving himself.

He reported to the principal's office as that was where he was asked to be as the school hadn't made up its mind where to host his lecture. Damian was surprised when the principal walked with him to the gymnasium. He was more surprised when he saw that it was filled to capacity with students and their parents.

He stopped at the door and asked, "Are you sure this is the right room? Is there a game about to start?"

The principal smiled and said, "Yes, this is the room. When you set the time with the computer club, word traveled and before we knew it, most of the senior class wanted to be here as well as their parents. You have to understand, you're a superhero that saved the students' and their parents' ambitions for college.

Damian paused a moment longer at the door and sighed. This was a different audience than he planned. He decided to discuss it with the assembled group. He also looked around to see if Hermione was in the bleacher seating, but he didn't see her.

He saw that the school had provided his requested materials, namely a screen, a projector, and an adapter for his computer. He walked in thinking about how to change the presentation when everyone stood up and gave him a standing ovation. Damian understood what it was for, but he hated this kind of attention. He would have to ask Hermione if she knew of the audience change in his presentation. He waited for the applause to die down and people to take their seats.

He started to address the audience, "I guess you all know who I am, but I'll still introduce myself. Hermione Knowles is my ward, and she came home from school and told me about the problem of your missing transcripts. She's worked at my company in the summertime and knows that I am a computer geek of the highest level. She told me about the problem here with the additional expectation that I solve the problem within two weeks to meet the college application deadlines. Then she went to her room to work on her homework."

Several parents in the audience chuckled and directed knowing glances at their teenagers.

"So I turned up at the school the next day and offered to work on the problem while the district went to work finding a computer expert to solve the problem. The school moved forward on a two-pronged approach," Damian said, his ego strong enough that he didn't feel the need to point out that he was the best and cheapest option to fix their problem.

"I had a presentation with me for the computer science club and I can tell by the number of people here, that this is not the club. So if you lack the computer geek gene, my presentation may be boring or indecipherable and you may want to leave now."

Damian waited, but no one got up and left the gymnasium.

"Wow, I'll have to tell Mr. Stewart who heads the computer club that his club has grown in leaps and bounds."

Again, he got laughter for that comment as it was clear that most of the people in the room were not intending to join the computer club.

Damian began his presentation with an overview of what happened to data when you tried to delete it. He also gave an introduction to the dark web and provided the parents in the audience with instructions on how to prevent their teen from going there. From there he talked about how he sought out a data set with Hermione's name, another student, and the science teacher.

"The hacker clearly believed the school didn't have the resources to chase down his hack and I found the data with relative ease. I also set up a protocol for subsequent classes. The IT department will save the transcripts in three areas, so if an outside force gets into the grading system, they school will have two other sources."

He saw relieved facial expressions when he noted that other grades of the school would be safe-guarded.

"I'll take questions now."

Several parents asked for written instructions on how to keep their teenager out of the dark web. Damian indicated that he would send them to the school, and they could distribute the instructions to all parents.

"Do you know why the school was hacked and who did it?" one of the parents asked.

"The hacker lived in Malaysia and I don't know why they did it. They are out of reach of the American justice system, but the school is protected from future hackers." Damian had been dreading the question as he didn't want to admit that Hermione's real parents were in protective custody and the hacker was hired by the company that had been trying to kill them for quite some time. He'd thought for a while the previous night and had come up with this answer.

He was ready to close out his appearance when one of the parents stood up and said, "I probably speak for many parents in this room, when I say that you saved my child's future. We had a few days of nail biting when we were sure our dream of sending our child off to college looked bleak. My son knew your daughter and she promised that you would fix the transcript problem in time. Her confidence in you helped us maintain hope in those dark hours. So thanks to her and you for getting us back on track to chase our college dreams again."

When she finished speaking, another round of applause and a standing ovation took place. Damian acknowledged the woman's words and then went about disconnecting his laptop from the school so he could escape. Before he made it to the door, there was a wall of parents wanting to thank him personally. Damian couldn't wait to get to his boat parked at Ariana's dock and the fresh air of a cruise across the bay. He never liked to be the focus of attention, and there was so much emotion in the gymnasium. He made his escape about fifteen minutes later and hustled to Ariana's SUV, shutting the door and heaving a sigh of relief. He headed for her home and more importantly the dock.

# CHAPTER 14

*D*amian pointed his boat toward his island. He made a quick stop to top off the cat food and proceeded on to the marina and his office. His employees knew he was going to be late and were curious as to how his presentation went.

"Actually, I was terrorized. I thought I was lecturing to perhaps fifteen students from the computer club. Instead, the school invited the entire senior class and their parents, and it was in a filled gymnasium. As you can imagine, I had to quickly change course. I ended up demonstrating to the parents how to block their child from reaching the dark web."

"Oh my," Haley said.

"I promise that you'll face a much smaller audience at Jacob's school," Lily said. "Can you give me the handout on the dark web? I need to stay one step in front of Jacob."

"Will do. I feel like I need a Pete's cheeseburger and a beer after this morning. Does anyone want to dine with me?"

His entire crew joined in the restaurant on the bottom floor of his warehouse. He was surprised with himself—he thought himself peopled out after his presentation that morning. Really, what he needed was a chance to wind down with people who knew him well and with whom he had worked for the past two years.

After lunch he opened his computer for the first time since the presentation at the school that morning. There were emails from Dr. Jill Quint and Sara Baldwin. He opened Sara's email first, hoping against hope that she had saved telephone records from the year her husband died. A long time ago, your telephone bill consisted of local and long-distance phone calls that you were charged for. Now most people had unlimited calling anywhere within their home country and phone bills were delivered by email. It appeared to be Damian's lucky day—Sara had kept the phone bill from the month that he died. She was sentimental about that being some of the last things that he did before he passed. She had scanned the bill and attached it to the email.

Damian leaned back in his chair and threw his arms into the air feeling victorious for this new piece of information. He copied the phone numbers into a separate spreadsheet and then had his computer identify the owners of those telephone numbers. As his computer was running through that data, he opened Dr. Quint's email. She had suggestions for several fast-acting poisons that Ryan Alexander could have given to John Baldwin in a flask. Her top guesses were arsenic, atropine, strychnine, and cyanide. Thallium was also a fast-acting poison in that it quickly made you sick but it took a few days to kill you. Her favorite was cyanide as it wouldn't be too difficult to obtain. The killer would also have the added advantage of the cold destroying some evidence in John's remains. Next, he started searching for where you could procure cyanide. There were many places you could buy it, so it would not have been a problem for Ryan to obtain the poison. She further commented that any of her listed poisons could still be tested for if a flask was ever found even though ten years had passed. In fact, if John was buried, his remains would show cyanide poisoning.

Damian went back and looked at his notes on the case and as he thought, John was cremated, so there was never going to be evidence from his remains. They could test his ashes, but something like that would never hold sway in court due to contamination in the crematory chamber. As Detective Severino would say, Ryan Alexander had the means, the motive, and the opportunity to kill his co-founder, John Baldwin.

His computer beeped, indicating it was done searching for the owner identification of the various telephone numbers. He looked through the list and spotted many calls from wife Sara and partner Ryan. There was nothing unusual about that. There were no calls from Ryan on the day of John's death, which was unusual. The partners had spoken at least once every day. However, there was an unknown number that conversed with John twice on the day he died. Damian would bet that it was a burner phone—the kind you bought from a big box store and activated it with a prepaid card. It would be hard to connect the two, especially if the buyer of the phone used cash to make their purchase. One of the calls occurred around about an hour before John's estimated time of death. Still, while he had lots of ideas about what happened to John, he had no proof of anything.

What if he was wrong about everything? Maybe John died at the hand of random person? No, that reasoning was false as evidenced by the lack of ski tracks leading to the position of his body. He was definitely murdered. Who else wanted him dead? He used his software to search the domain emails again, but this time he looked for use of exclamation points and the words *can't* and *won't* as that would point to emotion in the content of the emails.

Sunnyside AI worked with a couple of local wineries to test their technology with them. Some of the winery owners were frustrated with the app not providing exactly what they wanted, but those were minor conversations. The company let go of an employee who had an attendance problem, and the employee was unhappy about that, but not enough to kill. Besides, he couldn't imagine John accepting an invitation from that ex-employee to go cross-country skiing in Lake Tahoe. Then he thought of the spouse—wasn't it always supposed to be the spouse? He needed to eliminate Sara.

He pulled up the initial reports of the investigation. Detectives verified that Sara was in the San Jose area at the time of her husband's death. He hadn't thought she could be the killer, but it was always good to have his intuition verified by facts.

It was back to Ryan Alexander. Damian sat there staring off into space and thinking about finding new evidence. Another email arrived from Natalie with follow up from the attempted invasion of Sara Baldwin's house. They caught one of the intruders and another one they caught on the film of the drone that one of her sons had used to chase the man down. Both men had criminal records including for assault and battery. Damian wondered if they were sent to the residence to kill or threaten Sara. He sent that question to Natalie as he hadn't seen the answer to his question in her email. She did provide the names of the perpetrators in hopes that Damian could connect them to Ryan or any other suspect that they had.

Damian looked at the time and realized he had to get back across the bay as Hermione had another match this afternoon in about an hour. So he dashed out of the office and to the marina. He made a quick stop at his island to grab clothes and feed the cats before heading out for Ariana's dock. He managed to unload his stuff and drive to school for the second home match. After this game, the next three games would be away at other schools, but due to the lateness of the hour he left work, he was glad this game was at home. He walked inside the pool area and got the camera and tripod set up just as they were introducing the players on each team. He saw Hermione smile at his flustered last-minute arrival. Then he retreated to the stands, where several parents acknowledged him. They seemed friendlier than usual.

He took a seat to watch the action. He was dying to run some computer checks, but he thought that keeping his eyes on the phone rather than the game was rude—he came to support his ward during her game and so he should pay attention. He would scan his emails in case any new information came along from the detective, but otherwise he kept his focus on the game. At halftime, he got up to stop the recording of the game. When he sat back down, several parents came over to chat with him. Most parents were in their own little bubble during these games, so Damian had never spoken much with any of them before today.

"I never connected the guy who records games to the parent who could search the dark web and save my child's future. I thought you were the audio-visual guy, not the brilliant IT person," one mother said.

"I can be both. Mostly I'm the parent that cheers on Hermione."

A couple of other parents said much the same thing to him. A few asked after Ariana as the two of them were most often together at these games. Then halftime was over, and it was back to the pool. He started the recording the game again. Hermione's team won again. It wasn't so much a brilliant half-time speech by their coach as the other team was weak. Once again, Hermione wanted to eat out after the game and so they planned to meet up at their favorite Mexican restaurant.

Damian naturally arrived first. This time he didn't order for Hermione as she had many favorites at this restaurant. She arrived fifteen minutes later with wet hair and a big appetite. They discussed the game for a little bit and then moved on to the computer club presentation.

"How did your presentation go to the computer club?"

"Ha. You set me up. You knew the principal opened it up to your entire class and someone forgot to tell me."

"Yeah, I knew that was going to happen, but I didn't think it would matter, so I forgot to tell you."

"How come you didn't attend?"

"I already knew everything about the problem. They canceled our classes so every senior student could attend. I used the time to go to the library and work on a paper due for my history class."

"That a good reason."

"Were the parents not happy with your presentation?" the teenager asked, confused as to why Damian was unhappy about not knowing about the venue change.

"They were so happy they gave me two standing ovations. It was embarrassing."

Hermione grinned and said, "I bet it was. Here you were just undoing the damage by the Malaysians seeking to cause harm to my parents and me, and suddenly the whole senior class and their parents are giving you a standing ovation. But to be fair, it did take a computer genius to find our transcripts and fix the problem. So even if I was the cause of the problem, you were definitely the genius who fixed it. Your actions saved the college future for like five hundred kids. That's pretty heroic even if I was the cause of the initial problem. Also, did you follow the hacker beyond Malaysia to see who hired them? Maybe it was completely unrelated to me."

"True that your name or that of your parents was not connected to the arrangement I found, but among like twenty thousand high schools in America, why did your high school class get so lucky?"

"Someone had to get lucky," Hermione said with a smile.

Damian was glad that Hermione wasn't taking responsibility for the heist of her high school class transcripts. It wasn't her fault, and he was glad she could see that.

His Friday was quiet other than the presentation to Jacob's class. It went the way he'd expected the first presentation to go—he had a small class of geeks who wanted more details about the dark web than he was willing to explain. Damian spent the weekend at Ariana's house with quick visits twice a day to his island to take care of his cats. Hermione joined for at least one visit each day. Ariana returned late Sunday, tired from the long flight from the East Coast to the West Coast and the three-hour time difference. Damian congratulated her on obtaining funding for one of her start-ups. She laughed when she learned that Hermione and the school had set up Damian for the surprise presentation in the auditorium. Damian was tempted to stay the night, but Ariana was tired, and he had neglected things at home so he could be there for Hermione. He boated home and was glad to be back in his own bed. The cats were happy to be back in his bed with him. He had taken notes on a few things to follow up on the next day regarding the death of John Baldwin.

After his normal morning swim around the island, he started a few runs on his computer and then left for the office. On his list of things to do was follow up on any DNA on John's clothing, take another look at Ryan Alexander's bank records, find a certain seed-funding presentation, and review Ryan's social media posts.

Once he arrived at the office, he looked through Natalie's emails about the evidence that the police department had kept for John Baldwin's death? Did they still have any of his personal possessions from the time of his death? Some of the items were returned to his wife and Damian would bet that she hadn't kept his ski jacket or even ski equipment from that time. He thought back to what he had from Jen and the girls. When he finished this house and prepared to move into it, he'd taken the time to go through their belongings at the time and consolidated their lives into a few cardboard boxes that were in his laboratory. He hadn't kept any of the girls' sporting equipment or clothing, choosing to donate everything somewhere where someone could use it. It had been depressing when he sat back and realized his marriage of ten years and his offspring had been reduced to the pitiful collection of boxes. Those boxes represented his second grieving period which came two years after the original hit to his soul.

When he reviewed the list from Natalie, all that was in the possession of the police was a DNA swab result for a piece of tissue that was found near John's body. At the time, there was no match for it in the system. He emailed Natalie asking her to put it through again for a match. Ryan likely had no DNA in the system, but one never knew. John Baldwin's evidence had been reduced to this piece of tissue paper, and that was indeed sad.

Next he returned to Ryan's bank accounts. He wondered if he had all the accounts. He should be able to spot the payment to the fake attorney and maybe the thug who tried to break onto his island. At the time of his partner's death, Ryan hadn't been smart enough to use a different credit card to pay for his drive to Lake Tahoe, but now perhaps he was more careful.

Damian reviewed the records for his private banking as well as that for the company. He seemed just arrogant enough to use company funds to hire a hitman to take on Damian.

Chasing financial records sent Damian down a rabbit hole, but eventually toward the end of the day, he thought he had managed to collect all possible accounts from two years before John's death to the present. He would study the accounts the next day. He was packing up for the day, having managed to balance his employees' needs with this unlimited curiosity to examine any details about Ryan Alexander.

Natalie called just as he was leaving the marina for his island. He answered his phone though he was shouting over the sound of the wind. "Natalie, can I call you back in ten minutes? I'm close to my island and the wind is so loud, I'm having a hard time hearing you." He thought he heard a yes from her and ended the call, turning the boat toward home. When he arrived, he brought the boat inside his water craft garage, and pulled up the dock. He knew that a thug would be back at some point to take him on, and he wasn't going to make it easy for them. He sat down at his laboratory computer and put the call through to Natalie.

"Hey Natalie, what's up?"

"I just wanted to let you know that I did resubmit the paper tissue sample found at the crime scene and the DNA is still unmatched. Ryan's DNA is not in the system, so this doesn't rule him in or out."

"I guess I'm not surprised about that. I looked through the crime scene reports, and it appears that at the time of John's death, not a lot was done to collect evidence as both police departments had not declared his case a homicide. Is that correct on my part?"

"That about sums it up. Nearly all the personal effects were returned to his wife. I can't imagine that she kept old ski equipment from a decade ago."

"I was thinking through that idea myself. My life with Jen and the girls has been reduced to three cardboard boxes in my lower-level laboratory. It was very depressing at the time and still is today."

"I'm sorry, Damian. Have you opened up any of the boxes to remind yourself of your memories?"

"Not in the past five years. There seems to be no point going over the stuff. It just leaves me with a bigger hole in my heart."

"Ah," Natalie said, not knowing just what to say.

Damian thought it was time to move on to a different topic and asked, "So what are you working on for this case? I lost track of that at some point."

"I've been interviewing past co-workers and acquaintances of our suspect. No one has had anything nice to say. We're also investigating the suspect from your island break-in attempt. We would rather get both of them on something far bigger than what we have now. We have both of them under surveillance. Your intruder has been inactive; we think it's because he's waiting for the green dye to fade."

"It's kind of hard to be a bright green thug. It's like Nickelodeon is shining a spotlight on your thugly activities."

Natalie laughed at his description, "That's a great description. I almost wish we could dye all our offenders. Run them through a green slime shower before booking them. Alas, from my time watching that show with my kids, that green slime washes off, unlike your dye job."

"Okay, thanks for the update. I'm brain dead for the day, so I'm not planning any new research tonight. I think I'll take the evening off and just watch the baseball game tonight. I'll get back to research tomorrow."

They exchanged their goodbyes, and he soon found himself with a nice cup of tea and a stir-fry mishmash of things that were in his refrigerator that he was worried about spoiling. It was a nice evening. It had been a stressful week between assuming full-time parenting for Hermione, to meeting the parents at her school, and ending it thinking about Jen and the girls.

As he tended toward melancholy at times, when he examined his life, he asked himself if he was living up to his pledge to Jen and the girls to make the world a better place. He thought about his work with Natalie and his company and thought they would be pleased about that. He liked to think that his daughters would have been friends with Hermione. She had arrived with a good moral backbone, and he and Ariana had done nothing to weaken the fact that she was a good person.

Bella and Bailey were stretched out beside him on the couch enjoying a tummy rub like they hadn't had in a few weeks due to his absences. No, he decided, there was nothing he could do better for any of the people in his life. He tuned back into the game only to find that the San Francisco Giants were losing. They weren't going to go far into the World Series race if they didn't get their act together in this game. He shut the game off and retired to bed.

He woke up the next morning to word that another assault had been made against Sara Baldwin's house, and again it was easily thwarted per Natalie. The assailants were in police custody and Sara and the boys were fine. Damian had come into their lives at the right moment. Meanwhile, Marcus Blackstone was pushing for a settlement to agitate Ryan Alexander and get what he felt Sara was denied a decade ago at the time of her husband's death.

A quick thought passed over Damian that Jen would have greatly approved of his actions to protect Sara. The security enhancements had been paid for out of his own pocket, and he would not be reimbursed, but he had the satisfaction of knowing that she and the boys were safe, and their future would be secured between the security and the lawyer help that he connected them to.

He arrived at his office excited to return to reviewing the things he had on his checklist. He searched for one of the early seed-funding presentations where he noted that the venture capital company requested that Ryan be replaced. They saw him as a barrier to the company's success. John and Ryan rejected the company's demands, but he wondered what the investors saw during the presentation that turned them off so much to Ryan Alexander.

He'd made copies of the presentations when he visited the Wayback Machine at the museum. He just needed to find that particular one on his phone. He uploaded all the presentations to his main computer, then used the larger screen to sort through them quickly. He landed on the one with the concerns about Ryan Alexander. It was rare that comments were written on these decks about the people presenting the idea. If there were comments in the pitch decks that the museum collected, it was about the invention, not the people. Finally he found the pitch deck in question and Damian checked the name on it. He reviewed the history of funding for Grape AI and noted that this particular private equity firm chose not to fund the company over leadership concerns. Whoever had written in the margin said that *co-founder Ryan Alexander had zero interest in receiving feedback on their idea, and that would hamper the company going forward.*

It was an interesting comment. He looked at the date of the presentation and it was about two months before John's death. He wondered if that feedback is what put the events in motion that led to his demise. He looked for the names of the private equity firm attendees and then proceeded to search for where they were now. Some investors jumped from firm to firm and others left to form new partnerships with different investment strategies. It took some time, but he figured out who likely had been in the room during the presentation, and he sought them out to see if they would remember any part of the presentation.

It was a long shot, but perhaps it was the triggering event. He left messages for the relevant parties and then went back to work.

He looked into Ryan's finances, but now it was time to focus on his green slime thug who tried to reach his island as well as those detained by the SJPD for approaching Sara Baldwin's house. He also wondered how Ryan found the thug—it's not like he could post on social media that he was looking for someone to do his dirty work. He looked back over his notes from Natalie to collect the names of those who had been arrested. With a total of four of them, surely he would find a connection back to Ryan. The trick was finding bank information, then breaking into each account. It was easier with a corporation; he could always find someone gullible enough to provide the secrets he sought. The other problem was the thugs had fairly common names, so he needed to do some work to find the accounts that aligned with those for whom he was searching.

His phone rang with an unrecognized number, but Damian answered it as it might be one of the investors he'd reached out to for the Sunnyside AI pitch deck.

"May I speak with Damian Green?"

"Speaking."

"Hi, this is Josh Vaughn and you left me a message asking me to call. I don't guess this call is about funding for one of your inventions?"

Damian chuckled, "Sorry to get your hopes up, but no, that's not my strategy. I like to create a working product, then sell it and collect royalties on the intellectual property. My company will be at the CES in January and I'm looking to sell the production rights to two of my latest inventions. I left you a message as I have a question for you dating back a decade about a company called Sunnyside AI."

"You do realize I have listened to hundreds if not thousands of pitch decks in the past decade? I don't recall that one off the top of my head, so my company must not have provided funding."

"I'll refresh your memory. It was an app to help vineyards. It was later renamed Grape AI. You listened to a pitch from the two co-founders—John Baldwin and Ryan Alexander. You wrote on the pitch deck that the company had no future with Ryan Alexander as a co-founder as he had zero ability to take feedback."

"You might be surprised at how often I run into problems with start-up companies. Next to a bad idea, it's the second most frequent reason I'll reject a pitch. I don't remember this particular company, but give me a moment and I'll look them up. Are you thinking of investing with them?"

"No. Shortly after you listened to the pitch, the other co-founder was murdered in Lake Tahoe. At the time of his death, police had insufficient evidence to label his death as a homicide, but in my spare time I work with a retired detective assigned to cold cases in the San Jose Police Department, and now the case has been reclassified as suspicious. You know a little of me as an inventor, but I also have extensive cloud-computing capacity to sort through data that assists with these cold cases. We have a suspect in this case, but there is not enough evidence yet for an arrest or anything else. I wanted to talk with you about your impression of the two co-founders and perhaps understand why you chose not to provide funding. As I mentioned the company changed its name and a few years later did an IPO that raised millions."

"I didn't track the company, but it sounds like I missed an opportunity with it. Is Ryan Alexander still involved?"

"He is, and the company got funding not long after their presentation to you. It was just after the death of the other co-founder, and they were on the rocks with just days to being shut down. The company that did provide seed funding demanded approval of a new engineer as a requirement for their funding, and I think that saved the company. So you weren't wrong with the problems you saw and heard during the pitch presentation."

"Okay. Well this sounds like a very curious situation and I'll have to say I'm happy you can use your computing experience to serve law enforcement. I'm going to take a look at the old pitch deck and if I see anything that we didn't discuss during this call, I'll let you know. By the way, where did you find my notes?"

"That pitch deck is archived at the Wayback Machine at the Tech Museum. So your comments are preserved for posterity there."

"I didn't know that. I obviously know of the Wayback Machine, but I guess I never really thought about how pitch decks got added to it, let alone one with my handwritten notes on it. I guess one of my partners at the time thought it should be saved for the future."

"Yes. I'm not sure what gets saved by the museum and what goes into the rubbish pile."

"Are you sure you're not looking to pitch any of your inventions to my firm?"

Damian smiled, "I'm sure, but like I said, you're welcome to make an offer for some of my inventions but know that you'll have to take the product into production as part of the offer. I don't invent things just to have them end up on someone's shelf collecting dust."

They wrapped up their conversation with Josh promising to provide any feedback he found about Sunnyside AI.

Damian had just leaned back in his chair, when he heard a window break in their warehouse followed by an explosion. He was out of his chair in an instant and running to check on his employees.

# CHAPTER 16

Damian walked into the large workspace and tried to see through the dust in the air.

"Anyone here, anyone injured?" he called out.

Haley and Chris were crawling out from under a lab table with dust and debris on them.

"What happened? Are you injured?" Damian asked.

"We were running tests, and a brick came sailing through that window," Haley said pointing to the window and then looking around for the brick on the floor. She also pointed to her ears and said in a loud volume, "My hearing is gone at the moment."

Damian hoped the damage was only temporary.

"Given our last experience with an explosion here, we immediately took cover, and the lab table protected us from the explosion caused by what I guess is a grenade," Chris said. "So we're dirty, and deaf, but not injured."

"Dang. I think it's this case with Grape AI. I'm helping someone get their rightful share of an IPO and it's likely going to cost that company around fifty million dollars," Damian said, hearing sirens coming toward the warehouse. "I'm going to check that everyone else is okay. Haley, would you call or text your mother-in-law and assure her you're safe and report what happened here? As there might be evidence in here, why don't you guys leave this area to the police?"

She pointed to her ear, so Damian wrote her a note. She nodded and pulled out her cellphone while following Damian out of the damaged area. The remainder of his staff were apparently dining downstairs at Pete's and came rushing up to help.

"What happened?" Angus asked.

"Someone threw a brick in the window and then a grenade. Thankfully, Haley and I reacted by taking shelter under our lab tables and we're just dirty and deaf," Chris replied.

Damian did a quick count and all of his employees were there and safe. He heard the sound of an emergency vehicle approaching and decided it was time to send his staff home and start the cleanup process.

"Looks guys, I'm thrilled that you're all safe and I'm sorry I put your lives at risk. Just as soon as you give any eyewitness accounts to law enforcement, you're free to leave for the day. I'll clean this up and hopefully we can reopen tomorrow."

He heard comments like, "not your fault," and "we'll help clean up," and then there was chaos as police and fire units arrived on the scene. The emergency responders ordered everyone out of the building, including Pete's restaurant which was at the tail end of the lunch service. Damian thought he would be able to reopen for dinner as there appeared to be no damage to that area of the building as long as the police and fire cleared the area. He texted Ariana about the explosion as he might not make Hermione's water polo match depending on his cleanup effort required at the warehouse.

Fortunately, a survey of the building showed that the damage was much less extensive than first thought. The grenade was a flash bang which caused debris to fly, but didn't cause any real demolition. Haley and Chris might have trouble hearing for a few hours, but otherwise with a little cleanup and a new window, the warehouse would be functional the next day. Damian was standing on the outside looking at the building and thinking about putting bars over the windows to prevent more actions like this since it was the second time that someone had tried to damage his warehouse. He wished he could fortify the building like his house, but with Pete's restaurant being a busy and public use of the building, he couldn't do that. He thought about installing bullet proof glass, but that would take time and he was sure if it could repel grenades.

A few hours later, he was given the all-clear. The upstairs window was boarded up until the glass company could replace it the next day. He and a few of the employees cleaned up the mess from the flash bang and they had everything put back in place in time for Damian to leave and make the water polo match. The detectives from Richmond collaborated with Natalie on suspects. He provided the video coverage from the building, and using his facial recognition software had the suspect identified, and the Richmond police started searching for the suspect.

On his way to Hermione's game, he thought about Ryan Alexander. By attacking Damian's staff and his place of business, he'd made it personal, and it appeared that he was becoming more desperate. Besides letting the wheels of justice grind slowly, what else could he do to link Ryan with these attacks and with John Baldwin's murder? So far he hadn't found any evidence of payment between him and any thugs. Was he paying people in cash? How much did a thug get paid for trying to destroy Damian's home and work, or attacking Sara and the boys? Given that if you're caught, it's time in prison, it was likely at least a fifty- thousand-dollar job. He forwarded his thoughts about the situation to Natalie. Maybe the police would learn something about the payment during their interview process.

He arrived at Ariana's, and they quickly exited her garage to drive to a competitor high school that was hosting Hermione's team. He updated her on the way there and only just managed to get the camera set up for the game. He sat down on the pool bleachers sighing relief that he'd made it. It was a competitive match with the other team leading at the half. Damian hoped that Hermione's coach would give another excellent halftime speech.

"Did you notice why Hermione's team is behind?" Damian asked Ariana.

"Yes. They keep sending the ball to a forward who is striking at the left side of the net and the other team's goalie is left-handed, so she's blocking all the shots. They need to hit the other side of the net."

"Wow, that's a great analysis. Let's hope the coach noticed that too. He's been pretty good at the half time speeches."

They chatted with a few other parents and then the break was over and the teams back in the pool. Damian watched the player that Ariana pointed out and saw her change tactics and the ball was spread among more players, all attacking the right side of the net. They tied the score, and it stayed that way until the final minute of the game, when Hermione's team took the lead. It was an exciting finish. They made eye contact with Hermione and she grinned, giving them a thumbs up meaning she would meet them at her favorite pizza restaurant.

After they were seated at the pizza joint, Damian said, "I'm amazed that the child can eat as much pizza as she does and as frequently as she does. I'm so bored with pizza."

"It's a comfort food—win or lose, pizza brings her comfort," Ariana said.

"So I just need to suck it up and enjoy a slice?"

"Exactly. Are you going to tell her about the flash bang today?"

"Yes," he said, as he noted Hermione enter the restaurant.

The pizza was already ordered, and the soft drink glass was on her placemat waiting for her to fill it. She grabbed it, filled it, drank almost the whole cup, then refilled it and returned to the table.

"So what did your coach say after the game was over?" Ariana asked.

"He thanked us for listening to him at the half. I think sometimes that there is so much water splashing in front of our eyes that we can't see the forest for the trees."

Damian nodded as Ariana asked, "Did he tell you to stop aiming for the left side of the net at the half?"

"He did. I think everyone saw what was wrong, but we couldn't change our behavior without coach telling us. Kind of stupid, but hey, we're only high school kids."

Ariana and Damian smiled at the teenager, then he added, "I like how you seem to keep all problems in perspective."

"When you've been on the run to avoid kidnapping, then you don't get worked up about a water polo match."

"Oh Sweetie!" Ariana said, moving over to hug Hermione.

Damian put his hand on hers and said, "Kiddo, I'm so proud of you."

"Enough! I can't have my guardians getting emotional on me. Do you guys need to see a therapist?"

Ariana and Damian chuckled and shook their heads thinking about how wonderful this teenager was. Damian decided it was time to change the subject.

"So Kiddo, you know that I've been working a cold case with the SJPD, right?"

Hermione nodded.

"So someone threw a brick through the warehouse window and then followed that with a flash bang grenade today."

"OMG. Were any of your employees hurt? I can see you're fine."

"No one was hurt, though Haley and Chris might not have

their full hearing back for a few days. The warehouse is already cleaned up, the window is boarded up, and Pete's restaurant should be serving the dinner crowd."

"That's all good news. Tell me what's going on with the cold case. I've been so involved with school, sports, and college applications that I haven't been paying attention to what else is happening."

Damian summarized the case for her and what he was doing as they finished their pizza.

"Have you tried looking at the replacement engineer to see what they're up to?"

Damian was impressed with how Hermione zeroed in on the one aspect he hadn't paid attention to.

"I mean, it seems like you searched everyone else, but if this engineer replaced the dead guy and he's stayed with your horrible CEO for a decade, then isn't he corrupt too?"

"I can see I should have brought you in on the investigation at the start. You're right; everyone who was nice and decent has deserted the company and that can only mean one reason for the engineer to still be there. I'll check into his background when I arrive home tonight."

They soon wrapped up dinner, drove home to Ariana's, and then Damian was moving across San Francisco Bay at night excited about the prospect of something new to research for the case.

The engineer's name was Aaron Cooper; when Damian did a deep dive into the background of Cooper, he couldn't believe what he found. He was grateful for Hermione's suggestion that he look at the man.

# CHAPTER 17

$\mathcal{M}$r. Cooper was a replica of Ryan Alexander. Historically, his marriage broke up like Ryan's. People didn't like working for him either as the turnover was over 100 percent annually. There were out-of-court settlements for harassment and poor ratings of the company on Glassdoor. Damian took a quick look at the IPO offering and saw that it had made Aaron rich. With that information, he had a motive to plot with Ryan against John Baldwin.

Damian looked at Cooper's background and while he knew the concept of software coding, he didn't know enough to program the software for Grape AI. Which was why Damian found it so easy to prove that Sara Baldwin was owed a large part of the IPO proceeds. So far he had been focused on Ryan Alexander as the potential murderer of John Baldwin, but what if the two of them conspired to move John out and replace him with Aaron? From a timing perspective, it appeared that that's what happened. The product that was on the market today was nearly exactly what it was at the time of the launch ten years ago.

Damien had thought one of the investors had placed the

engineer in the company. However, now that he understood Aaron Cooper's coding talent, he doubted that was correct. He needed to look into how Ryan and Aaron met or maybe he needed to look at how all three men came together. He set his computer to work looking for interactions among the three men going back twenty to thirty years. As it was getting late and he knew that he could stay awake all night pursuing answers, he decided to shut down his work for the night. It wasn't like the two men were going anywhere, so whether he found the answer now or the next day didn't really matter with this case.

He went upstairs and decided to do some nighttime fishing for the cats. He found it relaxing to sit on the edge of his island with Bella and Bailey nearby watching his fishing pole. It was the perfect brain cleanser so he could shut down his thoughts and get some sleep. He perched on his favorite rock and had a lantern nearby so he could see what he was doing. He looked out across San Francisco Bay at the lights of the city and the bridges. At this hour there were no ferries in the water. There were big ships in the distance headed for the ports at Oakland and San Francisco. He'd pulled two fish out of the Bay and into his bucket of water when he heard his perimeter alarms go off on his phone. What now?

Damien grabbed the bucket of fish and his equipment and walked toward his front door. Given his past experience with people attacking his island, he left the fish bucket tucked away in some rocks about twenty feet from the door. That way if they tried to shoot up the front door, the cat's meal would not go to waste. He convinced the cats to follow him into the house and headed downstairs to his laboratory. So much for trying to relax before he went to sleep.

He opened his security programs to see what had set off the alarms. There was a drone headed his way. He traced it back to a boat sitting in the Bay. Apparently, the thugs were getting smarter and knew to stay some distance from the island. He wondered what the drone was carrying. He launched his own drone to get a better look and to take it out of the sky. His favorite tactic was to use honey on the enemy drone which gummed up its works and caused it to fall on his island. Given his experience with the flash bang earlier that day if the drone was carrying a flash bang or other type of grenade, he would rather drown it in the bay. His house was designed to survive a drone attack, still the island itself was made of a type of rock that would splinter during an explosion. He also launched a second drone to investigate the boat and see who was on board. He could drop one of his signature green slime balloons on them.

He briefly thought about calling law enforcement, but he thought he could handle this best himself and he might collect some evidence linking Aaron and Ryan to the attack. His first drone met the incoming drone on the edge of his island and doused it with honey. It sunk into the water and then there was an explosion of water and rocks where it landed. The drone pilot must have detonated something. He had video footage of the explosion, but whether he had any evidence left on his island he wouldn't be able to determine until daylight tomorrow. Meanwhile, the boat had turned around and was heading back to shore. Damian chased it with his second drone, knowing the pilot of the boat would be unable to hear it over the sound of the wind and waves. Damian smiled when he got the drone about a foot over his assailant's head and then he hit the button to release the green slime water balloon on his head. The boat swerved as the thug was briefly blinded by the liquid running down his face, and then Damian let go of a chuckle as he watched the man spread the green slime as he tried to clear his vision. He raised the drone and backed off the boat, intending to see which harbor the boat headed for to dock. He took a look at the pictures he'd snapped of the boat's occupant, but given the darkness and camera angle, he didn't end up with any decent pictures. Depending on which harbor he headed for, Damian could follow with the drone, but his range was just over ten miles. If the boat was docked in San Francisco, he would be unable to track it as it was beyond his drone's range.

As he continued to follow the boat, he smiled when he saw it heading for a dock in the Berkeley marina. He maneuvered the drone to try to capture an image of the boater, but despite the lights of the marina it was still too dark to get a good image. He snapped a picture of the call letters on the boat and then pulled the drone home. Then he changed his mind and decided to follow the guy to whatever vehicle he had parked near the marina. If he had a license plate, maybe that would identify him. The marina had rocks everywhere and hopefully the noise of the lapping waves on those rocks would cover the sound that his drone made. He followed the dude to a car and snapped a picture of the license, and this time brought the drone back to the island for the night.

He took a few moments to send pictures to Natalie in hopes that the detective could identify his assailant either through the car license plate or a boat rental agreement. Regardless, he wouldn't have answers tonight. He went back outside to his bucket of fish and took them over to the outdoor station where he quickly had them filleted and ready for the cats' midnight treat and morning breakfast. A short time later he settled into bed with some meditative deep breaths and fell asleep.

The next morning he took care of breakfast for himself and the cats and headed over to his warehouse to meet with the glass company. He knew he had new data about Aaron Cooper to look at on his computer, but he needed to secure his company first. He checked in with Pete, who confirmed that he lost minimal business yesterday.

"You know, Damian, when I chose this location, I didn't expect all of the excitement that comes with people trying to maim you."

"Yes, sorry about that, Pete. My inventor brain is trying to figure out how to protect the warehouse but allow the public access to your restaurant. Still, I love having you on site and I'm glad you didn't lose much business yesterday."

"It's all good. The neighborhood was talking about the incident, and I have more reservations today than yesterday. You made a minor celebrity out of my restaurant."

Damian nodded and went outside to greet the glass company people. They would measure this morning and install later today.

"You know, I replaced the glass here last year. Your company must not be well liked."

"Actually, it's not the company, it's me personally that the thugs are after. Do you have any ideas about how to stop the next grenade being launched at my office that would still be aesthetically pleasing?"

"Wow, who do you keep pissing off?"

"I do side work for the police department, and in both cases, it was the suspect who thought his case would go away if I did."

"Since you're still here, I'm thinking that didn't work out so well for them."

"Nope."

"We could add a fine mesh about two inches from the glass. It would stop rocks and bricks from breaking the glass, but not a grenade. From the inside looking out, it will look like a screen."

"Go ahead and do that for all the windows in this warehouse. While it is the same one that keeps getting broken, I may as well shore up all the windows."

The man nodded and walked away to take measurements. While he had been speaking to the glass man, his staff had arrived and listened.

"Thoughts? Do you think adding some protection to our windows will help? How's the hearing, Haley and Chris?"

"I'm back to hearing stuff. I think I got my hearing back last night," Haley said, and Chris nodded.

"I think the mesh protection will help a little. Certainly, the brick wouldn't have made it through, but the explosion from a grenade might destroy the mesh. Do you want us to go to the glass factory and test out their mesh before you pay to install it?" Angus asked.

"Normally I'd agree with you, Angus, that I should test something before I put it in place, but maybe this might visually deter people. The nice thing is I have cameras everywhere and we got all the suspects on film. Shall we go inside?"

His staff followed him inside and they all headed to the room with the boarded-up window. Everything was back in its place and the dust and debris from the flash bang was gone. Except for the blocked window, it looked like every other day at work. After assuring himself that his staff were okay and good with the situation, he retreated to his office to see what his computer search had turned up on Aaron Cooper.

Half an hour later, he thought he had the whole scenario wrong in his head. He still thought that Ryan Alexander was the likely murderer of John Baldwin, but he thought it likely that Aaron Cooper was the mastermind rather than Ryan Alexander. The only thing he hadn't figured out was how Aaron had gotten hired. He knew that most of the venture capital firms that had listened to pitches from John and Ryan saw Ryan as a liability. So the question for him was why they thought Aaron Cooper, who knew of coding but couldn't do it for a complex app like Grape AI, would have been approved by a seed-funding company. So what was the connection between that seed funder and Aaron?

A further search revealed the answer for him. They were college students together at Stanford. So did the seed funder end up with a special deal when the company offered its IPO? These three men seemed like the worst of the software bros, which was an ugly type of human being that inhabited Silicon Valley. Bros, typically male and full of themselves, only looked out for one another while everyone else was someone to screw financially or ethically or from an intellectual property perspective. As he was about to do a deeper dive into their relationships, his phone rang, and he saw from the caller ID it was Natalie.

"How are you and the warehouse doing this morning?"

"We're back to normal. Haley said she got her hearing back last night, which is good news. I'm adding mesh in front of my windows which will stop bricks from being tossed through the glass, but if someone wants to take a grenade or sniper rifle to this business, they'll still have the capacity to do that. I would add a lot more protection to the building, but I can only go so far with Pete's restaurant operating here. From a security point of view, having that restaurant be a part of the warehouse was a bad decision on my part. That said, both my staff and I really appreciate having good food nearby. So if I had it to do all over again, maybe I would have bought the building across the street and put the restaurant there. Maybe if I stop helping the San Jose Police Department, my security won't be infringed upon anymore."

"On the plus side, having thugs attack your island and your business helps us find suspects sooner and gives us more charges for longer jail sentences. I just wish my daughter-in-law wasn't in the line of fire. If only we could get the thugs to attack the warehouse at night when there was no risk to the people inside."

"That's true but you've given me an idea. I could increase the security on the building for the hours that the restaurant is closed and that might help us see bad activity sooner. I think I'll do that for my own peace of mind. Has anyone found the flash bang thrower yet?"

"That's actually what I was calling to tell you about. With

your facial recognition we identified where this thug lives, and no surprise, it's in the same Oakland projects as the other thug lives in. Our BOLO hasn't found him yet, but I think we'll have him soon."

"How about the guy who attacked my island last night? Any background information on him? I did not get a good picture of him to be able to use my facial recognition software so I'm hopeful that the license plate or the boat rental turns something up for the police."

"Unfortunately, no. The license plate was stolen, and the boat rental was a fake name. Did you say you hit him with the green slime? Doesn't your green slime have GPS crystals in it?"

Damian banged his head against his desk at his own stupidity. "I was so caught up into researching the engineer named Aaron Cooper that I forgot about the capabilities of my green slime. I must be losing my mind. Just a moment while I trace where he is located at this time."

Damien banged his head again, this time against his palm wondering how he had forgotten about the GPS crystals in his slime. Using the software program connected to the crystals, he located the guy in Oakland and gave Natalie the address. She would have to coordinate with a different police department to pick the man up. Fortunately, he had filmed the whole adventure last night and the police could use that to charge the suspect. He ended the call with Natalie and again pounded his forehead with his palm at his own stupidity to forget about the GPS crystals.

"Do you have a headache?" Lily asked from his doorway.

"No. Just an incredible few hours of stupidity. I can't remember the last time my brain let me down so badly. I'm trying to shake it back into shape."

"Hey, Super-brainiac, we all forget important details at times. Cut yourself some slack. What did you forget?"

"Another thug tried to visit my island last night. I doused

him in the green slime solution but then forgot that I could trace his location for the next three days. I just gave his location to the police, so hopefully he'll be under arrest soon."

"In the scheme of the world, does it make a difference whether he got arrested last night or today?"

"Probably not. Since he's covered in green dye, I can't see him committing any crimes until it fades as it is too much of an identifier."

"Then give yourself grace and let it go."

"I'm probably not ready to let it go. Last night I used my drone to follow the thug's boat to the Berkeley marina. I could have just traced the crystals and gone to sleep knowing the police would find the dude."

"What else were you doing at that hour besides defending your home?"

"Ah, I was fishing fresh fish for my cats."

"And what else?"

"I was doing a computer search on the engineer who took over for the guy who died in my cold case as I now think he's involved with John Baldwin's murder."

"You also were thinking about this building getting blown up and you probably were thinking about something with Ariana and Hermione. I still say it again, cut yourself some slack."

"Okay, okay. Can I help you with something?"

"I just wanted you to know that I found the person to help with my repetitive testing. I forwarded her information to Ariana and all the paperwork has been completed. She'll be here tomorrow. Would you like to meet her?"

"Yes. You know I need to make my customary speech about confidentiality as well as welcome her to the crew. What's her name?"

"Grace Yang. She's a statistics student at Berkeley."

"Make sure Pete has her name to add to our food bill."

"Will do, and I'll bring her by to meet you in the morning."

"Thanks Lily, and thanks for the pep talk. As you said, it's hard being a Super-brainiac, then realizing I forgot something basic to one of my inventions," Damian said with a wry grin.

She nodded and disappeared.

Damian returned to the search for more information about the software bros. It was time to hack into the accounts of the seed investor, whose name was Thomas Brogan, and Aaron Cooper to see what gains they had made with the IPO and if any payments occurred between them and any of the thugs. Also, he would try to rule them out as potential killers of John Baldwin.

# CHAPTER 18

*I*n between checking on his staff and their projects, and being distracted by the glass people, it took Damian the remainder of the day to break into the finances of both men. Then he needed to dig further as they had offshore accounts. It took a while to see they had set up a group and individual accounts in different Cayman Islands banks. Damian called it quits in the evening when he realized he had hours of work ahead of him breaking into the banks. He also planned to take a leaf out of prior efforts to expose banking secrets and look into the law firms that set up the shell corporations. He updated Natalie on his efforts and focus.

He thought about what he would do with the evidence once he found it. As he was illegally obtaining it, the legal system would be unable to use it for prosecution. Also, he wanted Sara Baldwin to get her share of the IPO proceeds before he tanked the Grape AI company, and he knew it would tank once word of the leadership's actions was available for the world to see. He decided to reach out to Marcus for advice.

"Hey Damian, what's up? Normally, I can guess why a client

is calling me, but you have so many irons in different fires that I don't bother guessing with you."

"I think I need to meet with you on a hiking trail or somewhere else where I can be absolutely sure that no one can listen. I trust you and your attorney-client privilege, but I have a feeling of paranoia at the moment."

"Wow, that sounds intriguing. I could come out to your island. Surely you've rendered that soundproof."

"Geez, that's the second time today that I've missed the obvious answer. Are you available this evening? I can pick you up in Richmond or Berkeley by boat."

"No helicopter?"

"Nope. There's room to land on my island, but I don't own a copter."

"I have a friend who does. Let me see if he'll fly me there as he owes me a favor. I'm afraid that with traffic, I'll otherwise be two to three hours reaching your location."

"Okay, let me know. He can stay in his copter or if he's a fisherman, he can go fishing while we're discussing my issues. If he doesn't like bay fish, he can fish for my cats' food."

Marcus chuckled at that and said, "I'll let you know."

By the time he reached his home half an hour later, he received word from Marcus that he would be arriving by helicopter in about an hour. His pilot friend would take Damian up on fishing for his cats. Damian pulled out a few homemade pizzas from his freezer. Then he smiled when he thought about the fact he was turning into Hermione by eating pizza twice in one week. While he was waiting for Marcus to arrive, he decided to call Ariana.

"Hey there, how's your day going?" she asked.

"I remember about four years ago, when I never left my island and just invented things in my basement laboratory. In the last twenty-four hours, I've dropped green slime on another intruder, put new windows and a protective mesh in front of all my warehouse windows, and discovered a deeper conspiracy than I expected in my cold case. Also, as Lily called me "Super-brainiac," I've been let down by said brain twice as well. How's your day been?"

"Downright boring compared to your exciting life," she said with a chuckle. "There's been no excitement in my or Hermione's life for a few days. She did mention that she asked her parents about what was happening with their court case. They're getting close to the end, and they've testified. They are going to pass on to the judge the incident with her high school hacking in hopes that will add financial penalties to the case."

"Tell her to pass on to her parents that I have proof of the connection to their court case if they need it."

"Will do. Do you need our help defending your island? We do like a good game of 'Drown the Red Rock Island intruder' with your water cannons."

Damian thought this was just another reason he loved this woman. There was no drama, just an offer to help.

"Actually, my attorney Marcus Blackstone is on his way here in a helicopter. I'm about to do something illegal and wanted his advice. I suggested we meet on a hiking path, and he suggested coming to the island. Like duh, this is one place I don't need to worry about anyone overhearing my conversation."

"Ah, that must have been one of your Super-brainiac failures."

"It was. The other was I forgot to track the intruder who was wearing my green slime-GPS crystals mix last night. Fortunately, Natalie asked about it and so law enforcement should be close to picking him up."

"Dang, the cop knew your inventions better than you did. That must have caused you to eat a slice of humble pie," she said through the laughter.

"I ate a large slice of humble pie. I face-palmed my brain so many times that Lily asked if I had a headache. Thanks for taking care of the paperwork to hire Grace Yang, by the way."

"You're welcome. Wait till I tell Hermione about your mistakes. She might lower you from where you sit atop Mount Everest as the smartest man on Earth to just Mount Whitney heights."

"Thanks for that, I needed a laugh about my mistakes today."

"Call me back after Marcus leaves so I know how much bail is going to cost me when you go to jail for whatever you plan to do illegally. Just ask him for an amount, okay?"

Damian relaxed further after laughing at Ariana's practical questions about his situation. Then he heard his perimeter sensors alarming and thought the helicopter might be getting close.

"Will do, I think he's arriving. I'll call you later on our burner phones." It always paid to be paranoid and to know where to avoid possible holes in his security.

They ended the call, and he switched over to see what had set off his alarms. Indeed, it was a helicopter. He could only hope it was a friendly one. He was grateful it was still daylight as he could see Marcus in the front seat. He walked outside to greet him. The helicopter landed on the flat surface not far from his fish-cleaning station. The rotors stopped moving and Marcus got out of the helicopter to walk over to Damian.

"My friend decided he didn't like the wind currents here— he's afraid it might turn his bird on its side. He's going to head over to land and sit there until I need him."

"I don't blame him. I had an enemy helicopter land last year and it took a special crane to get the rental helicopter off my island," Damian said as the two men waved the helicopter off.

"For a nerdy inventor, you do live an adventurous life. Someday you'll have to tell me about the enemy helicopter over a beer, but let's go over your planned illegal activity."

"I pulled a couple of homemade pizzas out of my freezer if you would like to eat while we discuss my issues."

"Sounds like a plan if you have beer to wash the pizza down with as the two go together in my world."

"I can fulfill that request," Damian said, opening his front door.

"I've always been curious about your house. Tell me about it while you heat the pizza."

Damian told him about the design and features of the house and island over cold beer and gave him a tour of both levels, the watercraft garage, as well as the chairlift from his beach.

"I would have said you're paranoid with all the materials and security that you have here, but now that I understand the law enforcement response time and the problems you've had here with bad actors, this seems like a perfectly planned space. So tell me what you're planning to do illegally so I can advise you not to do it."

Damian smiled at that last piece of advice, "I actually have two asks of you. I'm going to tank the company, Grape AI, but I'd like Sara Baldwin to get her money first. Are you at all close to a settlement, and if not, could you use the threat of bad publicity to force the settlement? I also understand I'm asking you privileged information but . . ."

"I guess that whatever illegal thing you plan to do, something will devalue Grape AI. Why don't you tell me the second part of your ask, and then I'll have a better sense of what I can do to settle the matter."

"So you know that I've been working with the SJPD to solve the death of Sara's husband, who was the engineer who designed Grape AI, or Sunnyside AI as it was called at the time. I think his death was part of a conspiracy among a seed investor named Thomas Brogan, an engineer by the name of Aaron Cooper who replaced John, and the current CEO Ryan Alexander. The three of them are software bros and were students together at Stanford."

"As I've gotten further in my legal career, I've learned to spot software bros, and I refuse to work with them. Every last one of them is a liar, and there are few things I hate more than having a client lie to me," Marcus said before biting into a slice of pizza.

"Yeah, well they recognized they had a great product on the backs of John's work. A decade ago they set up joint and individual accounts in the Cayman Islands. I'm convinced that I'll be able to follow the money and find where they have hired the thugs who have been attacking Sara and me. I also think they have been skimming profits from the company. Finally. I think that if these three are not in jail, Sara will continue to be a target because that's the way they work."

"So your problem is that you're illegally hacking into their systems to find this information, right?"

"Yes. I was looking at the Panama Papers as an example to follow. The law firm that was at the heart of that scandal dissolved after all the negative publicity that they aided clients in doing all kinds of illegal things. I've identified the law firm that assisted with these three in setting up these offshore accounts and I'm sure I can break into their records. I'm also trying to find the whereabouts of Cooper and Brogan at the time that John died, and that information will be illegally obtained by hacking into their personal financial records. I know that Ryan was in the Lake Tahoe region around the time of John's death, but at this point that means nothing to law enforcement as far as proving he was John's murderer. I may not be able to prove that, but if I can find a bunch of financial crimes that will put him in jail and cause him to lose control of the company, that's almost as good."

"So you want to know how to anonymously expose the software bros that will force the government to take action and collapse the company, but you want Sara to get her share first."

"Yes. How do I go about doing that?"

"Wow, you know I'm a patent attorney, not a criminal or financial crimes legal eagle," Marcus said.

"You said it, you're a legal eagle. How do I proceed?"

"I think I would follow the same path as the Panama Papers and dump the information on journalists. The question is, which journalists? The Panama Papers were an international scandal. Here you're talking about a software company and Silicon Valley bros. So maybe look at the San Francisco Gazette or the San Jose Crescent or both to see who bites. The problem will be that those news sources will need to verify your findings. Did you look at how the journalists did that for the Panama Papers?"

"The journalists worked on it for six months before they began releasing stories about the data leak. One German journalist knows who the leaker is but has kept that a secret as his life is at risk. Putin put an amount of money on his head for the leak. In my case, I'm not worried about my personal security, but I don't want to be charged with hacking."

"Okay, let me see first if I can force a settlement from Grape AI tomorrow. They'll balk at resolving the lawsuit on such short notice, but I'll threaten to go to the press about how poorly Sara was treated by the company and the fact her husband's product is essentially unchanged. I'll check with Sara as I think we'll need to settle for a lower number—say forty million versus fifty million—but I think she'll approve. That should cause some wineries to walk away, and their stock to tank. Of course, we'll have to sign an agreement not to reveal these facts to the world, which we'll do, but that won't stop you. I'll even write up a press release to increase the threat. I'll also give you the name of a good defense lawyer in case you have to make that call."

"Yeah, Ariana asked me to ask you how much my bail would be, so she knows how much she has to raise," Damian said with a smile.

"That's a wise woman. As an attorney it's my duty to advise you not to do anything illegal, but I understand your position with this intriguing case. I wish you every success and will be cheering secretly from the side lines. By the way, I assume the detective you're working with on this case won't give you away as the hacker. That's likely your weakest link."

"I think the SJPD will claim ignorance of me and my activities as they know they have solved all kinds of cases with the retired detective's and my help. They routinely ask me to be their employee. Also, from what I've read about hackers who have been caught, all police departments lack the technical expertise to figure out who the hackers are and catch them. As I'm not skimming credit cards or extorting Grape AI, they can't be bothered with me."

"Okay, it sounds like you have a good plan. I'll let you know when we've settled. Are you ready to go right now and share information with journalists?"

"No. I need to do a little more research, then tie it up in a neat bow for the journalists to be able to follow. I probably have about two weeks of work in front of me."

"That's good to know. I want to see the wire transfer of payment from Grape AI, then you can put the software bros out of business. Will this cause a problem for the wineries?"

"It will, but Grape AI has been unable to hold onto coding staff and has made only superficial software updates. There's another company called Wine-Barrel+ that is making its mark in the industry and taking clients away from Grape AI. They will likely buy out Grape AI after its fire sale."

"I can see you've done your research," Marcus said.

"I don't know what it is about me that makes me so mad about injustices. A member of my staff called me Super-brainiac this morning and I guess that suits me. I ride my computer data to seek justice."

"I like that title. I can see you in a Marvel movie holding out your keyboard and mouse to defend those being treated unfairly by software bros," Marcus said with a smile. "Let me know when your story is on the big screen so I can watch."

"If I have my way, only you and the Grape AI threesome will ever suspect but will not be able to prove who was behind the company's downfall."

They wrapped up their conversation and went outside to await the return of the helicopter. After it left, Damian returned inside and updated Ariana. He also set up a meeting with Natalie in a few days to explain where he was going with the case. The police department was picking off the minor criminals involved in the case, but he was after the software bros.

# CHAPTER 19

$\mathcal{M}$arcus worked his legal magic, and a week later, the wire transfer of forty million dollars from Grape AI hit the attorney's bank account that he'd set up for the purpose. Sara Baldwin was set for life. Now, Damian was free to take down the software bros.

A smirk curled at the corner of Damian's lips as he stretched back in his chair, cracking his knuckles. The real game was about to begin. Between Hermione's sports games, some much-needed downtime with Ariana, and leading his company, he had meticulously assembled a timeline, a damning data dump, and a compelling narrative. It was a story so explosive that no journalist worth their salt could ignore it—especially given the swirling rumors of John Baldwin's murder and the Silicon Valley empire built on deception.

He packaged the files carefully, encrypting them and creating an anonymous leak portal. His last move was to suggest to the journalists at both the San Francisco Gazette and the San Jose Crescent that they collaborate, hinting that a Pulitzer Prize might be in their future. He could almost hear the newsroom scramble the moment they accessed the files.

As expected, they wasted time trying to verify his identity. But Damian had covered his tracks well. He was a ghost providing them with a story, a shadow whispering the truth into the world's ear.

Three days later, the headlines screamed:

**EXCLUSIVE: GRAPE AI'S DARK SECRET—THE SOFT-WARE BROS, OFFSHORE FRAUD, AND A MURDER LINKED TO SILICON VALLEY GIANTS**

The financial world erupted. Stockholders panicked. The SEC launched an immediate investigation. The DOJ wasn't far behind.

But Damian wasn't done.

He met with Natalie at his house, ensuring complete privacy, and laid out the final pieces. While they could place Ryan Alexander, Thomas Brogan, and Aaron Cooper in Lake Tahoe at the time of John Baldwin's death, there was still no direct evidence linking them to his murder.

That changed two days later when police, armed with new financial crime charges and a growing mountain of evidence, raided Ryan Alexander's home.

The discovery was chilling.

Hidden in the humidor room, among his prized collection of expensive cigars and whiskey, lay a leather-bound flask. It seemed an odd trophy until forensic analysis confirmed what Damian had suspected all along.

The flask contained John Baldwin's DNA, and cyanide and arsenic. Just the poisons that Dr. Quint had suggested.

The murder weapon had been hiding in plain sight. A relic of Ryan's arrogance, a quiet testament to his own guilt. The arrest came swiftly. Caught in a whirlwind of corporate collapse, financial crimes, and now a murder charge, Ryan Alexander barely had time to process his downfall before he was marched out of his fancy house in handcuffs. Cameras flashed. Reporters shouted. Once he was booked, a DNA sample was taken. It matched the tissue found on the ground near John's body. That tissue that was kept in evidence for ten years sealed Ryan's fate.

At the police station, the real gamesmanship began. The three software bros cracked under pressure, turning on one another in a desperate bid to cut a deal. The threat of San Quentin was enough to break even the most arrogant of them.

Aaron Cooper and Thomas Brogan secured lesser sentences, their confessions further sealing Ryan's fate.

The trial was a media spectacle. The prosecution painted Ryan as a calculating manipulator, willing to kill to secure his dominance and fortune. The defense fought to discredit the evidence, but the truth had already been laid bare. The jury deliberated for less than a day before returning with a guilty verdict.

Life in prison. No parole. It was justice at last for John Baldwin and his family after ten long years of struggle.

Sara Baldwin and her boys moved out of state, far away from the shadows of Silicon Valley. Damian and Marcus met with her one last time before she left, ensuring that she had everything she needed for a fresh start. With Marcus's help, her share of Grape AI had been secured, protected, and managed by a different part of his firm—one that wouldn't betray her trust.

As for Damian, he turned his focus back to his company, to Ariana, to the life he had carefully built.

Most of the news about the software bros had quieted down by the end of the school year. Hermione was accepted to Berkeley and would start school there in the fall. Her parents' legal case was also winding its way through court, and they might be free to live their lives outside of witness protection in the near future.

He sat beside Ariana in the packed auditorium, watching with pride as Hermione stepped up to the podium. As the valedictorian of her class, she spoke with a voice that was steady and full of determination.

"We all have our battles to fight," she said. "And sometimes, justice isn't easy. But the truth always finds a way."

As the audience erupted into applause, Damian leaned closer to Ariana and whispered, "Maybe she should consider politics instead of law school."

Ariana smirked. "Or cybersecurity."

He chuckled, shaking his head. And if the world ever needed him again, . . . well, he'd always be watching.

The End

# ABOUT THE AUTHOR

I now reside in Wisconsin, though my first 24 stories were written while I lived in Northern California. My rescue dog and cat are my companions while I write. I love to travel, play sports, read, and drink wine and beer. I enjoy the diversity of the world and I'm always watching people and events for story ideas. All of my stories are generated by my imagination, I don't use AI to write books.

If you would like to sign up for my monthly blog and announcement of new books, please follow this link: https://www.AlecPecheBooks.com

While you're waiting for the next story, if you would be so kind as to leave a review for this book, that would be great. I appreciate all the feedback and support. Reviews buoy my spirits and stoke the fires of creativity.

Readers that sign up for my blog receive a free prequel novelette for the Jill Quint Series.

Long Delayed Justice

Emerald Bay Murder

**<u>Michelle Watson Series</u>**

Now You Don't See Me

Where Did She Go?

How Did She Get There?

**<u>Dog Humor</u>**

Eat, Play, Poop: Letters to my parents from camp


**<u>A. Peche</u>**


**<u>New Urban Fantasy Series - Stephanie Jones</u>**

The Awakening at Lake Tahoe (short story)

Witch's Medicine

Witch's Quest (2025)